MW00755725

NO LON
FULLER

John Banville
Birchwood

John Banville was born in Wexford, Ireland, in
1945. The author of thirteen previous novels, he
has been the recipient of the James Tait Black
Memorial Prize, the *Guardian* Fiction Prize, a
Lannan Literary Award for Fiction, and, most recently, the Man Booker Prize. He lives in Dublin.

FULLERTON PUBLIC LIBRARY
HUNT BRANCH
201 SOUTH BASQUE
FULLERTON, CA 92633

ALSO BY JOHN BANVILLE

Birchwood

John Banville

VINTAGE INTERNATIONAL

Vintage Books

A Division of Random House, Inc.

New York

To the Dunham-Shermans
Stepan-Candaus, and
the Browns

FIRST VINTAGE INTERNATIONAL EDITION, MAY 2007

Copyright © 1973 by John Banville

All rights reserved. Published in the United States by
Vintage Books, a division of Random House, Inc., New York.
Originally published in Great Britain by Martin Secker &
Warburg Limited, London, and subsequently in hardcover in
the United States by W. W. Norton and Company, Inc.,
New York, in 1973.

Vintage is a registered trademark and Vintage International
and colophon are trademarks of Random House, Inc.

This is a work of fiction. Names, characters, places, and
incidents either are the product of the author's imagination
or are used fictitiously. Any resemblance to actual persons,
living or dead, events, or locales is entirely coincidental.

Cataloging-in-Publication Data is on file
at the Library of Congress.

Vintage ISBN: 978-0-307-27912-5

www.vintagebooks.com

Printed in the United States of America
10 9 8 7 6 5 4 3 2 1

PART I

The Book of the Dead

Odi et amo: quare id faciam, fortasse requiris.
  Nescio, sed fieri sentio et excrucior.

I hate and I love; ask how? I cannot tell you
  Only I feel it, and I am torn in two.

CATULLUS

I AM, therefore I think. That seems inescapable. In this lawless house I spend the nights poring over my memories, fingering them, like an impotent casanova his old love letters, sniffing the dusty scent of violets. Some of these memories are in a language which I do not understand, the ones that could be headed, *the beginning of the old life*. They tell the story which I intend to copy here, all of it, if not its meaning, the story of the fall and rise of Birchwood, and of the part Sabatier and I played in the last battle.

The name is Godkin, Gabriel. I feel I have already lived for a century and more. This can only be an advantage. Am I mad, starting again, and like this? I have seen terrible things. It amazes me that I was allowed to survive to tell of them. Mad indeed.

And since all thinking is in a sense remembering, what, for instance, did I do in the womb, swimming there in those dim red waters with my past time still all before me? Intimations survive. Often a sound heard throbbing at dusk from the far side of a hill seems an echo of the wallop of their bellies as they coupled, heedless of their little mistakes already coming between them. This is nothing. In my time I have gone down twice to the same river. When I opened the shutters in the summerhouse by the lake a trembling disc of sunlight settled on the charred circle on the floor where Granny Godkin exploded. They must mean something, these extraordinary moments when the pig finds the truffle embedded in the muck.

I have begun to work on the house. Not that it is in need of repair, no. I swept away the broken glass, dead flowers, the other unnameable things. You would think I expect guests, which is a laugh. I fail to discern a defensible reason for my labours, but there must be one, I suppose, buried somewhere. It gives me something to do in these long dog days. At night I write, when Sirius rises in icy silence. The past is poised around me. I imagine an arrow whistling through the darkness.

I arrived in the spring. It was a glassy green morning, chill and bright. The sacks of the cart were wet, that smell stayed with me, and the smell of the horses too, big dull brown brutes stamping and pawing the road, throwing up their heads, their eyes flashing. The leaves of the trees in the wood sparkled, scarves of mist drifted among the branches. I looked down on the broken fountain, at last year's leaves sunk in the dead water. The windows of the house were blinded with light. Shadow and sunshine swept the garden, a bird whistled suddenly, piercingly, and in the surface of the pool below me a white cloud sailed into a blue bowl of sky.

The library is a long narrow room. Its dusty book-lined walls give way at the south end with a hint of gaiety to the white french windows that look across the lawn into the wood. Blackbirds hunted outside on the grass that day, thrushes too, frenetic little creatures with battle cries no bigger than themselves. There was a smell of lupins and, faintly, the sea. The windowpanes were smashed, withered leaves littered the carpet. The shards of shattered glass retained wedges of a stylised blue sky. The chairs crouched in menacing immobility. All these things, pretending to be dead. From the landing I looked down over the lake and the fields to the distant sea. How blue the water was, how yellow was the sun. A butterfly flickered across the garden. I strained to catch the tiny clatter such awkward wings should make. My fists were wet with tears. I was not weeping for those who were gone. People are easy to replace, thanks to their infamous proclivity. I wept for what was there and yet not there. For Birchwood.

We imagine that we remember things as they were, while in fact all we carry into the future are fragments which reconstruct a wholly illusory past. That first death we witness will always be a murmur of voices down a corridor and a clock falling silent in the darkened room, the end of love is forever two spent cigarettes in a saucer and a white door closing. I had dreamed of the house so often on my travels that now it refused to be real, even while I stood among its ruins. It was not Birchwood of which I had dreamed, but a dream of Birchwood, woven out of bits and scraps. On bright summer mornings the rooms were alive with a kind of quick silent suspense, the toys and teacups of the night before exactly as they were left and yet utterly changed. A moorhen's panic-stricken flight across the surface of the lake at evening seemed to crack the landscape in half. When the wind blew from the east the chimneys sang. These things, these madeleines, I gathered anew, compared them to my memories of them, added them to the mosaic, like an archaeologist mapping a buried empire. Still it eluded me, that thing-in-itself, and it was not until I ventured into the attics and the cellars, my favourite haunts, the forgotten corners, that the past at last blossomed in the present. I paused on the back stairs at twilight, by the potted palm before the door with the green glass panels, and the years were as nothing.

In this search for time misplaced I had great hopes for the photograph, one of the few things I brought away with me. Printed in yellowish brown tints, with a white crease aslant it like a bloodless vein, it was of a young girl dressed in white, standing in a garden, one hand resting lightly on the back of a wrought-iron seat. Mama said it was a picture of her as a child, but I could not believe that. Half of the scene was in sunlight, half in shade, and the girl with her eyes closed leaned from the dark into the light smiling blithely, dreamily, as though she were listening to some mysterious music. No, I knew this girl was someone else, a lost child, misplaced in time, and when I returned the picture had inexplicably altered, and would not fit into the new scheme of things, and I destroyed it.

Thus, always, I am surprised at the difference between the way things are and the way, before I find them, I expect them to be. For example, the vagina I had imagined as a nice neat hole, situated at the front, rather like a second navel, but less murky, a bright sun to the navel's surly moon. Judge then of my surprise and some fright when, in the evening wood, tumbling with Rosie through the lush wet grass, I fingered her furry damp secret and found not so much a hole as a wound, underneath, uncomfortably close to that other baleful orifice. That was how it was, coming home, always the unexpected.

Rosie was one thing, with her delicate gash, but that mighty maid whom many years later I met along the road! How she giggled and gasped, and kicked up her legs, trying to shake free from, or gobble up, I could not distinguish, that finger which plugged her so timidly. It must have been that chance encounter which left with me an abiding impression of the female as something like a kind of obese skeleton, a fine wire frame hung with pendulous fleshfruit, awkward, clumsy, frail in spite of its bulk, a motiveless wallowing juggernaut. Ach! In her too I discovered nooks and musty crannies, crevices which reminded me of nothing so much as the backwaters of the house where I had played as a child, that house which now sleeps around me as lightly as a bird while my stealthy pen blackens the pages. I have come into my inheritance. I think of that day high in the window when the tears fell for the first time, and I saw that figure on the lawn looking up at me with amusement and rage, the white knuckles, the eyes, the teeth, the flaming hair, these are the things we remember. Also I recall Silas and his band departing finally, the last caravans trundling down the drive. Did I spy, in the darkness of one of their poky windows, the glint of a merry eye regarding me? They went away, and when they were gone there was that creature in white, standing under the lilacs with a hand on the back of the seat, leaning into the sunlight, smiling, like one of Botticelli's maidens, and I can be forgiven for wondering if there were shrill trumpets in the distance, sounding their music through the earth and air.

MY FATHER IS grinning in his grave at the notion of his paltry son fiddling with this, with *his*, baroque madhouse. Mama in her plot is probably weeping. Birchwood for her was a kind of desert, bleak, magnificent, alien. She would have gladly seen the place collapse some suitably wet Sunday. In spring and summer, snatched from sleep by the raucous chorus of the birds, she would rise at dawn and wander through the corridors and the empty rooms, sighing, softly singing, a bit mad even then. On the day I arrived it was she who saw, through the window above the stove in the cavernous kitchen, Silas and the fat Angel coming up the drive. I wonder what she thought of when she saw them, what pestilence and passion? Though she cared nothing for our history, that glorious record of death and treachery of which the Godkins were so proud, it was that very history which made her life so difficult. She was a Lawless, and for such a sin there was no forgiveness.

The family tree is a curious one, with odd echoes among the branches and many an odd bird whistling in the leaves. For generations the Lawlesses were masters of Birchwood, and then my great-great-grandfather and namesake, Gabriel Godkin, arrived. Where he came from is not known, nor who he was. One day, suddenly, he was here, and nothing was the same again. Joseph Lawless, then squire of the estate, disappeared, died, was murdered, no matter. He is remembered in our annals for his answer to the commissioner who informed him at the height of a potato famine that the tenants of Birchwood were being decimated by starvation. *A trick, sir, another of their tricks!* Joseph roared.

7

Indeed he was right, was Joseph, for the peasants were a tricky lot, they died by the score, thereby forcing the authorities across the sea to send in a relief shipment of six sacks of Indian corn.

The estate was in ruin, bled white by agents and gombeen men. The land had been hacked into tiny holdings where the tenants were strangling the soil to death in their frantic efforts to meet the rents and feed their annually expanding families. All that was to change. Within six months of the, shall we say the disposal of the master, our Gabriel Godkin married the daughter of the house, Beatrice by name—echo!—and took over Birchwood. He broke up the smallholdings, and evicted those who would or could not fall in with his plans. He turned the estate into a huge collective farm ruled by his own ruthless though not unbenign despotism. While the tenants hated him for the loss of what they considered theirs, their own tiny plots, they relinquished their dignity, became serfs, and when their fellows in other parts were on their knees, cropping the grass, their own bellies were, if not full, at least not empty either.

At this point Gabriel's glory fades, he forfeits my interest. In the beginning a dark stranger appearing out of the south, touched with the magic of death and dreams, now he becomes merely another squire and country gent, a name in a parish register, a part of the past. Who was he? I do not know. I am not saying that I have no opinions, I have, but I keep them to myself, for reasons not entirely clear.

The Lawlesses, Joseph's brothers, fought for Birchwood, and what with the legal tangles, and the peculiarities of the will, not to mention the unshakeable faith in perfidy which there was on both sides, the fight was long and dirty in the extreme. Gabriel won, and his fortunes flourished. Demoralised by defeat, the Lawlesses languished. From landed stock to small-town merchants was a short step down. However, there is always justice, of a kind, and while the Lawlesses grew solid and sane the Godkins were stalked by an insatiable and glittering madness born, I suspect, of the need to hate something worthy of their hatred, a part the Lawlesses could no longer play. I am thinking of Simon Godkin furiously dying with his teeth sunk in birchbark, of my mother screaming in the attic. I am thinking of all the waste sad deaths. This violence will be visited on me, in the fullness of time.

My father's share of the family's congenital craziness took a novel and desperate form. He set himself to fall in love with Beatrice, daughter of John Michael Lawless and, correct me if I am wrong, the double-great-grandniece of Joseph, last of the Lawlesses at Birchwood. Papa, also called Joseph, another of those echoes bound to cause confusion, did not succeed in loving her, but married her all the same. Why? Did he have the guts to attack the Godkin madness at its root, end the feud, bring the Lawlesses home, complete the cycle begun a hundred years before? I doubt it. Perhaps he married Mama because his mother, my Granny Godkin, was so violently set against the match, and Joe was never one to pass up a fight with that ancient harridan, the only one of us that he loved, I hope that is the word. She could smell in this affair, she declared, a low plot on the part of the Lawlesses to regain Birchwood by the only means left open to them, namely, the tyranny of the cunt and its corollary, the womb. She may have been right. John Michael Lawless was a crafty old scoundrel behind the subservience, but if he held the deck in this game, the winning of which would see a transfer of business from his general store back to the great farm at Birchwood, he dealt the wrong cards to the wrong players. My father was not to be tyrannised, and poor Beatrice was no amazon, and any Lawless plot there might have been foundered finally on the tormented wasted love which Joseph so unexpectedly kindled in his bride.

He was a handsome man, with thick black hair brushed sternly back, a black moustache, and teeth like white stones. Who could have resisted him, with his weariness of spirit, his disenchantment, his wry gaiety? Beatrice imagined that it was these ill-perceived qualities combined which so pleasantly alarmed and excited her. She was mistaken. What she found fascinating in him, did she but know, was the muted but savage anguish that hounded him all his life, and which, in order to live with it, he transformed into fury or passion, brooding melancholy, visible pain. This is what she loved, by love's perverted nature, but if at first she found romantic an unhappiness which would not be alleviated by anything short of death, it was not long before she learned the folly of her notion. To live with one stricken by such a sickness is to experience compassion first and sympathy, then irritation, resentment, and finally a pity which is indistinguishable from revulsion. Romantic!

She hardly knew him, had seen him in the town, or riding the fields, had danced two foxtrots with him at a hunt ball, when she stopped on the stairs that winter morning and saw him in the hall with her father. Old Lawless stooped and simpered, clasping his hands on his breast, while Joseph leaned away from him with his jaw clenched in distaste. Though she made no sound he heard her, and turned.

'I want to marry you,' he said, just like that. Convulsed with embarrassment, she felt the blood rush to her face. She was not surprised, and that surprised her. They ignored her father's fulsome speechifying and went out and walked across the garden into the orchard. There, locked in silence, they stood under a bare black tree, and she watched, fascinated, Joseph slowly pulling off his gloves, finger by finger.

'Well?' he asked. 'What about it? I'm not going to kneel, you know.'

She said nothing, but flung herself at him. They grappled awkwardly in a stunned silence, her teeth clattering against his. He pushed her away, startled by her ferocity, and his hat fell off, he snatched it up, flashed his fierce cold grin with that gold tooth gleaming in it, turned quickly and stalked off through the trees. She found herself shivering, and noticed for the first time the bitter white cold in the air. He did not look back. The hoarfrost crackled under her slippers as she walked back to the house that was changed now beyond all recognition.

They were married in the spring. She wore white. In the church the window behind the altar blazed with light, scattering pale spangles around her on the flagstones. Baffled among the jumble of her emotions, she stumbled through the ceremony convinced that she was elsewhere. The wobbly music of the organ marched her out into the churchyard, where her heart stopped dead for an instant at the sight of the April sunlight shining gaily on the tombstones. Joseph suffered it all in a mood of tired boredom which he succeeded in enlivening only once, when he paused for a full five seconds before saying *Yes* to the contract. The minister gaped at him, nodding and mouthing in frantic dumb show, and Beatrice's mother, who was to die within the year, let loose a gulp of woe and slumped down in her invalid chair, and, for many years, Papa was to remember the occasion with a warm glow of spite.

The Lawlesses attended the wedding in force. They wept in the church, and stood solemnly to attention outside while their photographs were taken. At the reception they all got drunk, and Uncle Teddy, the rake, twirling his moustaches, sang questionable songs. They toasted the bride, and wept once more on each other's shoulders. The dining tables were taken away and they danced, and one of my aunts fell and broke her ankle. O they had a glorious time. Shopkeeping had made shopkeepers of them. The Godkins stayed away. Perhaps some of them really disapproved, but most of them were afraid to come for fear of Granny Godkin, who sat at home in the same chair all that long day long and planned a welcome for her son's bride at Birchwood.

What a welcome it was. They returned from blossoming Paris into rain, a wild sky, strife in the trees. The garden was sodden, the first flowers of the year scattered on the grass, soiled and broken. No fires were lit in the house. Joseph stamped through the rooms roaring for Josie the housekeeper, for his mother, for his dinner. Beatrice hauled their bags, plastered with wet yellow petals, into the hall, and wandered around the house, blowing her nose. In the drawing room she found Joseph, his mother and his sister Martha confronting each other, dumb with rage, all three. The old woman's eyes flickered toward the open door, where Mama hovered, and Joseph turned and stared at his wife with an icy eye.

'*Jesus*,' he muttered.

That was for her an ending of a kind. She had thought that life would be different and therefore better, but it was only different, and even the difference was not so great. She pondered the moments when all had seemed ready to change, but she could retrieve only bits and pieces, a tree in winter, smell of spring in a Paris street, bits and scraps. The real moments of transformation, these in time she forgot, long before, three seasons later, she looked from the kitchen and saw that rakish pair coming to plunder her morning.

TO BE SPECIFIC—to be specific!—what she saw or noticed first was the line of horsedrawn caravans halted outside on the road, their black roofs behind the hedge. Imagine her surprise, for it was not every day the traveller stopped at our forbidding gates, and, as if the caravans were not enough, she had next to cope with Silas and the fat woman. Silas was short and plump, with plump short legs and a big head, a big belly, and tufts of white hair sticking out under the brim of a black hat. He wore a black suit that was too tight for him, and white linen gloves. The fat woman's fat was trapped in a shapeless flowered dress with a crooked hem. A rainbow of feathers wobbled in her floppy hat. They paused to look up at the house, and Silas said something, and Angel laughed, and for a moment a kind of cruel ramshackle frivolity was abroad in the garden, like that in the instant between the steeplejack's stumble and his plummet to the cobbles when general laughter threatens to break out among the mourners gathered in the graveyard below. Arm in arm they set off again toward the front door, and soon Mama could no longer see them, though she leaned over the stove with her cheek pressed to the window. The bell rang insistently, and when she had swept through the dining room and the hall up to the first landing she saw them again, two grotesque foreshortened figures sitting calmly on the front steps with their faces turned to the garden. I think she was upset. What a predicament! She would not let them in. It was left to Josie, some time later, to open the door to them and reward their patience at last.

In the hall Angel sat on one of the little antique chairs inside the door, her arse overflowing the seat. Silas stood beside her with his hat held in his fingertips. Mama pressed her palms together and saw, on the sunlit step outside, a little black bird alight. Silas gazed at her in silence, with humour, with compassion, his head inclined. He peeled off one of his gloves and advanced, on tiptoe it seemed, and in the mirror of the hatless hatstand a plump smiling ghost appeared briefly. He offered her his chubby pink hand and murmured obsequious greetings. Angel opened her mouth and sneezed uproariously twice, her heels clattering on the parquet and her feathers wobbling. Silas and Mama ignored her, and she glared at them and sniffed haughtily. A tiny shadow darkened the doorway and the three of them ducked their heads as the bird flew into the hall, rose and turned with a wild whacking of wings and was gone. Silas laid a hand on his heart and turned again to Mama, his lips pursed, smiling at his own fright.

Such scenes as this I see, or imagine I see, no difference, through a glass sharply. The light is lucid, steady, and does not glance in spikes or stars from bright things, but shines in cool cubes, planes and violet lines and lines within planes, as light trapped in polished crystal will shine. Indeed, now that I think of it, I feel it is not a glass through which I see, but rather a gathering of perfect prisms. There is hardly any sound, except for now and then a faint ringing chime, or a distant twittering, strange, unsettling. Outside my memories, this silence and harmony, this brilliance I find again in that second silent world which exists, independent, ordered by unknown laws, in the depths of mirrors. This is how I remember such scenes. If I provide something otherwise than this, be assured that I am inventing.

Silas and Angel went back down the drive with a step jauntier than that which had brought them up, and soon the caravans came through the gateway and across the lawn down into the fallow field. There was shouting and laughter, and someone played a tin whistle. The horses when they were let loose wandered back to the lawn, searching out the sweet grass. A small boy, or he might have been a dwarf, came and hunted them away again. The whistle was joined by a bodhran. Mama stood and watched the camp take shape. The tall clock slowly tocked, and slender columns of shadow hung motionless from the ceiling behind her. At last she turned, and quickly, firmly, shut the door.

Granny Godkin lay awake, waiting, in the stuffy fastness of

13

her room. Her watchful silence unnerved Mama when she entered there each morning. Not the dawn over the fields began the day at Birchwood, but the first light breaking in Granny Godkin's bedroom. Mama drew the curtains. That was her task. Our house was run on ritual in those days. The old woman coughed and muttered, pretending to wake, and thrashed about under the blankets, until Mama set the pillow at the headboard and propped her against it.

'There you are now.'

'O, it's you.' Granny Godkin's dry cough rattled. 'Well?'

'Sun is out.'

'Good. Not a wink all night. Pains! What time is it?'

'Eight.'

'You took your time. My tea—?'

'On its way.'

This duet hardly varied from day to day. When it was finished they were lost. Mama drifted back to the window, while the old woman sat scratching the counterpane with her nails and turning her eyes vacantly from side to side. Theirs was a curious relationship. Granny Godkin, before she met her, had imagined Beatrice as a tough blue-eyed bitch. What a royal battle there would be! She polished her weapons and waited. That day of the wedding, when she sat staring into the garden, she burned with excitement. The real Beatrice, a gentle creature dazed by her passion for my father, was a bitter disappointment, but, refusing to give up her dreams of flying blood and hair, the old woman launched her attack regardless. Mama, mistaking what was expected of her, pretended that things were other than they were, made herself agreeable, replied to what she wanted to hear not what was said, smiled, smiled, and raged in her dreams. Such tactics were unbeatable because of their innocence, and Granny Godkin, in baffled fury, turned on her son and cried, *She has no style, no style*! Joseph grinned, and lit a cigar, and strolled out into the garden. Something in his mother folded up, she took to grumbling, and began to die, and there at last she found her finest weapon, for Beatrice knew, without knowing how, that she was killing the old woman. Joseph, mildly amused, observed this unexpected turn in the tide of war, and when Beatrice guiltily spoke of his mother's decline he grinned at her too and said that she would never die, *not, my dear, so long as she has you*. Which might have proved true had not the house, weary of this wild old woman, finally turned on her and extinguished her itself.

There was a scratching at the bedroom door, and it opened wide enough to allow in Granda Godkin's wizened skull. My grandmother turned her face away from him. The ancient couple could not remember when they had last spoken to each other, which is not to say that they did not have their suspicions, although it often occurred to me that each may well have thought the other already dead and come back a spiteful and tenacious ghost. Still with only his head inside the room Granda Godkin winked at Mama, who had turned from the window in sudden alarm.

'In a pet today, are we, in a pet?' he inquired, and nodded toward his wife. He withdrew his head with its sprinkling of ginger hairs, and a rattle of phlegm in the corridor betrayed his secret laughter. He was a wicked little old man. Once again his pixie's face appeared, and he was already speaking when Mama began to shake her head at him in urgent mute appeal.

'I see the tinkers have moved in.'

Another retreat, another laugh, and this time the door closed. Granny Godkin's eyes and mouth flew open—

'*Where's that Josie?*' Mama muttered, and fled. She was in the corridor before the old woman began to bray. Josie's ragged gray head came up the stairs, and she stopped, slopping tea into the saucer, and turned her ear toward the commotion in the bedroom with a bleak little grin.

'What's wrong with her now?' she asked.

'Bring in the tea, Josie, bring it in,' her mistress answered wearily. Poor Mama.

She went out into the garden, into the stained light and the birdsong, and walked on the lawn by the edge of the wood. A wind from the sea lashed the tops of the trees together and made spinning patterns of the fallen may blossom on the grass. Nockter the gardener, a square hulk of a man, knelt in the flowerbeds uprooting the weeds that flourished among the violets.

'P-p-powerful day, ma'am.'

'Yes, glorious.'

He edged away from her and bent again to his task, nervous of her mad placid smile.

She sat on the iron seat in the little arbour under the lilacs. An early cricket ticked among the bluebells. She heard without hearing it the music fade down in the fallow field. All was still in her little chapel, while, outside, spring whistled in the leaves, the chimneys, ran shrieking through the long grass under the trees. Spring. Perceive the scene, how, how shall I say, how the day quivers between silence and that spring song, such moments are rare, when it seems, in spite of all, that it might be possible to forgive the world for all that it is not. Granny Godkin came across the lawn, her jaw shaking furiously. She was dressed in black, with a white brooch at her throat. At every other step she plunged her stick into the ground and wrenched it free behind her.

'*Tinkers !*' she cried. 'You let them in!'

Mama said nothing. The old woman sank down beside her on the seat.

'You let them in,' she sighed, mournful now, her thin shoulders drooping, her shoulder blades folded like withered wings. That switch from anger to weary sadness was a well-tried assault on Mama's soft heart, but Mama had no time now for the game. Something odd was going on, a lowering silence surrounded her. She looked about the garden with a wary eye and murmured absently,

'They're not tinkers. It's a circus. It might be nice. What harm…?'

'What harm ?' Granny Godkin shrieked. 'What *harm* ? Look!'

Cloudshadow swept across the fallow field, and through that gloom a ragged band came marching. There was a young man with a sullen mouth, two strange pale girls, the small boy or dwarf. Were the others there too, those women, grotesque figures ? Granny Godkin rose and brandished her stick at them, gobbling in fury and fright.

'O Jesus Mary and Joseph they'll murder us all!'

A flock of birds rose above the trees with a wild clatter of wings. Granny Godkin fled, and Mama folded her hands in her lap, and closed her eyes and smiled. Ruin and slaughter and blood, brickdust, a million blades of shattered glass, the rooftree splintering—the poppies! Suddenly I see them, like a field of blood!

That day was to be forever famous in the history of Birchwood, and justly so. An invasion, no less! Granny Godkin's shoulder was dislocated by the shotgun she fired off at the invaders. Granda Godkin locked himself into a lavatory, where he was found hours after the battle sitting paralysed on the bowl and frothing at the mouth. A policeman's skull was split by an ashplant. Beatrice laughed and laughed. And I was born.

Papa, hacking home at evening, met Nockter running down the road with the news. What a splendid figure he must have cut, my dark father, eyes staring and teeth bared as he thundered up the drive on his black steed, the hoofbeats, the gravel flying, his coattails cracking in the wind, that is a sight you will not see every day these days. He dismounted by the fountain, and threw down the reins, and in that sudden silence stopped and heard above him a cry, a kind of stricken cough, and in an upstairs window a naked child was lifted, shaking its little fists. There was another cry, weaker than the first, and when it stopped, and the echoes stopped, a hollow horn of silence sounded throughout the house.

A LINE of tall trees trembling, a crooked field dusted with flowers, and sunlit figures walking a long way off. The sea was near, a faint soothing voice. The grassy ground bore me up with an admirable firmness. A hawk high in the blue wheeled slowly in descending arcs around a spire of air. Distant laughter tinkled like the sound bits of glass make falling into water. The hawk halted in flight, wings whipping, poised, then plummeted to earth. A tiny squeal pierced the stillness like a cold steel needle. The bird rose again and struggled up the pale blue air.

'There you are,' Mama murmured, leaning over me, and a primrose slipped from the bunch choking in her fist and fell into my lap. 'I see you, Mister Man.'

That is, I think, the earliest memory of my latest life. What I remember best would be best forgotten, but the fragments that remain of the first years I guard with a jealousy which grows more frantic as I grow older, for I am forgetting them. Mama wore a long dress of fragile cream-coloured stuff and a yellow hat with a wide brim. Her fingers were stained with the dust of the flowers. There was dust on the road. A man on a high iron bicycle passed us by and gravely lifted his cap. Tall stalks of grass stood very straight and still in the tangled hedges.

'And when you are able you'll sing a song, won't you? And dance too, for your Mama, because you love her.' She spoke in a hushed voice, almost a sigh, imparting some great secret. This woman whom, in the innocence of my heart, I called my mother, she was...what? Tall, very slim, with very long fine brown hair which each morning she bound into a burnished knot at the nape of her neck and each night unbound again. There is in the dark past, like something in Rembrandt, a corner illuminated where her hair tumbles softly in silence around her shoulders in the yellow dust of lamplight. I remember her as neither young nor old, but thirtyish, you might say, awkward and yet graceful, with perfect hands, yes, graceful and awkward all at once, I cannot put it better than that. I think she had a beautiful face, long and narrow, as pale as paper, with big dark eyes which, years later, I would find watching me shyly, stunned with helpless love for such a peculiar unapproachable creature as myself. Words. I cannot see her. When I try I cannot see her, I mean I cannot find any solid shape of her, as I can of Granny Godkin for example, or of my father, those who vibrate in the mind like unavoidable stars. Mama seems to have left behind her nothing of her essential self. Only the things that surrounded her come back, imbued with her presence, a fair prospect of trees, a clenched glove, light at evening, a yellow hat settling softly, slowly, into a wash of sunlight on a green table. It is as if she did not die, but rather was dispersed like vapour into objects of more endurance than she could ever claim, as if indeed she never existed, not what we call existing.

A path leads down by wooded ways to the summerhouse by the lake. There Granny Godkin sat, at a table by the window above the water, a pale skull floating among the paler reflections of tree and sky on the glass. She spent most of her days there in the year's clement weather, but how she spent them was her secret, for she was never caught unawares, but as we caught her now, watchful and silent, a game of patience, her alibi, spread before her on the rubbed green felt.

'Ah come and give your poor Granny a kiss.'

I have no wish to make her seem an ogre, but her smile was awful, really awful, a sort of shattered leer. She smelled of peppermint and dust, and the jaw that I kissed trembled with ague. I had, I know not how, gained her—gained her regard, I wanted to say love, but the Godkins loved only those they could fight, and as yet I was too young for that. Perhaps she found in my infancy an echo of her own senility. For a while she babbled away at me, nodding and leering and prodding me with her talons in a clumsy imitation of tenderness, until I turned away from her, and she fell silent. Mama sat down on a wicker chair and dropped her hat on the table, and the old woman turned her attention to me again for one more try at squeezing some sign of fondness out of me.

'And tell me, tell me this, who do you love the best?'

I did not answer, for I was engrossed in the startling and menacing intricacy of a daddy-longlegs going mad against the glass in the corner of the window, which was a small coincidence, for soon I saw, beyond the spinning insect, my own long-legged daddy approaching through the wood. Granny Godkin saw him too, and gave a cold neat sniff. He closed the door softly behind him, and without looking at any of us paced slowly past the table with his thumbs in the pockets of his tight black waistcoat. He always seemed to me, even in his worst rages, preoccupied with some old bad joke. Once, in a row with Aunt Martha, when she had flung an ashtray at his head, he snapped his teeth abruptly shut in the middle of a howl of fury and turned on his heel and stalked out into the garden. We sat in silence and inexplicable horror and listened to his laughter booming in the flower-scented darkness outside, and I, cowering in my corner, felt my face grinning wildly, uncontrollably, at this intimation of splendour, of violence and of pain.

'Well?' said Granny Godkin calmly. 'Have you managed to put us in the poorhouse yet?'

Papa, whistling very softly, raised his eyebrows and glanced at her, but continued to pace. Mama became elaborately interested in her fingernails.

'Well?' the old woman asked again.

He stopped behind her and looked down at the cards, tapping his foot to the beat of a silent melody. 'Poorhouse?' he murmured absently. 'Black knave on the red queen.'

'Pah!'

The cards rattled, and Mama bit her lip apprehensively. My father carried a chair from the corner and sat down by the table with his hands on his knees. I leaned against Mama's shoulder. They were shaping up for a fight, I saw it in my father's playful flinty grin, in the convulsive snapping of Granny Godkin's jaw.

'Did you see that man, you know, what's-his-name?' Mama asked, making a vain stab at nonchalance.

Papa lit one of his small dark cigars. The smoke, a bluish dove, hovered for a moment over the table and then flew slowly up into the shadows.

'A very civil fellow,' he said. 'Very civil. Treated me to a feed of bacon and cabbage in Regan's. *I know, Mr Godkin, you're a man I can trust.*' Granny Godkin cackled briefly. 'I sold him the long meadow,' Papa added quietly.

We waited on Granny Godkin. She peered at the cards and shifted her dentures. Either she had not heard his last remark, or the significance of the words had not registered.

'Trust!' she said. 'Huh!'

There would be no fight, not today. Mama, one hand resting lightly on her knee, relaxed and leaned far back on the chair, lifting her face to the window and the tender blue sky. Granny Godkin, her thoughts gone all away, shuffled the cards and shuffled them, slower, and slower. They made a silky sound, the cards, falling together. My father, his long legs elegantly crossed, smoked in silence, his eyes hooded. The sun shone on the table, on Mama's yellow hat. It was pleasant there in the silence of the dusty little room, surrounded by deck chairs and straw hats and other ghosts of forgotten summers. Often now, late at night, or working in the house on rainy days, I feel something soft and persistent pressing in on me, and with sadness and joy I welcome back this scene, or others like it, suffused with summer and silence, another world. Forgetting all I know, I try to describe these things, and only then do I realise, yet again, that the past is incommunicable.

THE BUTTERFLIES CAME in swarms in early summer, small blues, delicate creatures. There must have been something in the wood that attracted them, or in the garden, some rare wild plant perhaps. We got used to them, and when they found their way even into the house, and fluttered awkwardly, like clockwork flowers, around our heads at the breakfast table, it was with the tiniest frown of irritation that Mama rose to open the window, murmuring *shoo, shoo*. They were easily killed, I mean it would have been easy to kill them, while they went about their business on the lupins and the roses, but I never knowingly destroyed one of them, I don't know why. Indeed, in time I became their protector, their patron and friend, and I would carry them, throbbing in my cupped hands, out of the hall before Josie arrived with her mop to kill them. When I released them from the steps their incredulous drunken leap from my palm made the summer airs over the garden seem suddenly lighter, gayer, and as delicately tinted as the skyblue silken dust they left smeared on my fingers. Not that I had any love for them, or even liking. I wanted to kill them, but I did not. Some days my teeth ached with the desire for wanton slaughter, but I would not allow myself the pleasure, treasuring my benificence, and knowing anyway that if the situation became desperate there was nothing to stop me taking a rolled-up newspaper into the wood one afternoon and bludgeoning to extinction a whole species of lepidoptera, small blues, while they frittered away the first glorious days of summer.

It was in summer too that I came into my kingdom. The calendar date is lost, but the occasion is still invested in my mind with the sonorous harmony of a more complex, less tangible combination of pure numbers. There was a clearing in the wood, not a clearing, but an open place under the sadly drooping, slender boughs of a big tree. Mama sat at the edge of a white cloth spread on the grass, reading a book and brushing imaginary flies away from her cheek. At her feet my father lay on his back with his hands behind his head, quite still, and yet managing to give the impression of bouncing restlessly, tensely, on the springy turf. I watched, fascinated, this curious phenomenon, but soon the shifting patterns of light and leaf on the cloth distracted me, and there was another distraction, which it took me a while to identify, and it was this, that Mama had not once in ten minutes turned a page of her book. That was very strange. At last Papa stood up, stretched himself ostentatiously, and yawned. Mama's lack of interest in her book grew more intense, if that is possible, and I caught her glancing sideways at him with that furtive, mournful, altogether lovesick look which already I had come to know so well. Patting the last of his yawn with three fingertips, he considered the top of her head, the inclined pale plane of her jaw, and then turned and sauntered off into the trees, whistling through his teeth, his hands in his pockets. Soon she put her book away and followed him, as I knew she would. I was forgotten.

Our wood was one of nature's cripples. It covered, I suppose, three or four acres of the worst land on the farm, a hillside sloping down crookedly to the untended nether edge of the stagnant pond we called a lake. Under a couple of feet of soil there was a bed of solid rock, that intractable granite for which the area is notorious. On this unfriendly host the trees grew wicked and deformed, some of them so terribly twisted that they crawled horizontally across the hill, their warped branches warring with the undergrowth, while behind them, at some distance, the roots they had struggled to put down were thrust up again by the rock, queer maimed things. Here too, on the swollen trunks, were lymphatic mushrooms flourishing in sodden moss, and other things, reddish glandular blobs which I called dwarfs' ears. It was a hideous, secretive and exciting place, I liked it there, and when, surfeited on the fetid air of the lower wood, I sought the sunlight above the hill, there on a high ridge, to lift my spirit, was the eponymous patch of birches, restless gay little trees which sang in summer, and in winter winds rattled together their bare branches as delicate as lace.

Left alone, I pulled pale stalks of grass from their sockets and crushed the soft flesh in my mouth. Timidly, almost unnoticed, there came breaking in upon me that music, palpable and tender, which a wood in summer makes, whose melody is always just beyond hearing, always enticing. Dreamily I wandered down through the trees, into the bluegreen gloom. Down there were flies, not the intricate translucent things which browsed among the birches, but vivid nightblue brutes with brittle bodies, swarming over the rot, and there were black birds too, under the bushes screaming. Somewhere afar a dog barked listlessly between precise pauses, and I heard the sound of an axe, and other sounds too numerous to name. I came to Cotter's place. This was a little house, in ruins, with everything gone under lyme grass and thorns but for one end wall with a fireplace halfway up it, and a shattered chimney with the black flue exposed, and over the fireplace a cracked mirror, a miracle of light, staring impassively over the tops of the trees. I never knew who Cotter was, but the name suggested...never mind. He was long gone now, and in what had been his kitchen, among the ferns that flourished there, a woman's pale hands clutched and loosed in languorous spasms a pale white arse bare below a hiked-up shirttail. She cried out softly under his thrusts, and, as I watched, a delicate arc of briar beside them, caught by a stray breeze, sprang up suddenly into the air, where two butterflies were gravely dancing. Lift your head! Look! The mirror's pale, unwavering, utterly silent gaze sent something like a deep black note booming through the wood's limpid song, and I felt, what shall I say, that I had discovered something awful and exquisite, of immense, unshakeable calm.

I wandered farther then, by unknown ways, and soon I heard Mama's voice hallooing here and there, each cry a little closer. I waited, and it was not long until she came hurrying down the hill, hands fluttering and her hair streaming behind her. She leaned over me, enfolding me in a tender weight of love and concern, murmuring incoherently into my ear, warm round words, swollen like kisses. Her cheeks burned. We found Papa pacing impatiently under the tree, kicking leaves and smoking a cigar. The picnic things were packed and stacked beside him. As we approached he bent to pick them up, and bending gave me that crooked sidelong sort of grin which is about the most I ever had from him by way of affection, which I always tried to avoid, and never could, it was so knowing, so penetrating and so cold. Mama was very busy, tying up her hair, taking things out of the basket only to put them back again, foothering around, as Granny Godkin would have said. The folded cloth slipped from under her arm and opened like an ungainly flower, and from out of its centre staggered a bruised blue butterfly. She paused, stood motionless for a moment, and then very slowly put her hands over her face and began to cry. 'Jesus,' said Papa, without any particular emotion, and walked away from us. For my part I was quite calm.

We straggled homeward. My father's long stride carried him far ahead of us, and he had to stop often and urge us on with weary silent stares. Mama laughed and chattered and exclaimed over the flowers in the hedge, trying by her gaiety to make the three of us doubt that outburst of tears. Her prattling irritated me. Full of the secret glimpsed under Cotter's wall, I carried myself carefully, like a patient floating blissfully on a drug, forgetful of the pain biding its time outside the vacuum. O I am not saying that I had discovered love, or what they call the facts of life, for I no more understood what I had seen than I understood Mama's tears, no, all I had found was the notion of—I shall call it harmony. How would I explain, I do not understand it, but it was as if in the deep wood's gloom I had recognised, in me all along, waiting, an empty place where I could put the most disparate things and they would hang together, not very elegantly, perhaps, or comfortably, but yet together, singing like seraphs.

So it was, as I walked up the drive, I perceived in my once familiar kingdom the subtle strains of this new music. The sun shone calmly on the garden, except in the corner by the swing where daffodils blazed like trumpetblasts. Josie was polishing an upstairs window, and the glass, awash with sky, shivered and billowed under the sweep of her cloth. We climbed the steps, into the hall, and Mama, pressing a hand to her forehead, dropped a bunch of primroses on a chair and swept away to her room. The cluster of bruised flowers came slowly asunder, one fell, another, and then half of them tumbled in a flurry to the carpet, and behind me the tall clock creaked and clicked, and struck a sonorous bronze chord. Listen, listen, if I know my world, which is doubtful, but if I do, I know it is chaotic, mean and vicious, with laws cast in the wrong moulds, a fair conception gone awry, in short an awful place, and yet, and yet a place capable of glory in those rare moments when a little light breaks forth, and something is not explained, not forgiven, but merely illuminated.

IT WAS ON WET DAYS that the house really came alive for me, like a ponderous gloomy Chinese puzzle, those interminable Sundays, for they were always Sunday, when a thin drizzle fell all day, washing the colours out of the world outside the windows until even the black trees and the grey grass faded behind the fogged glass. They gave me things to play with, toy soldiers and tin drums, a fierce red rocking-horse with flared nostrils. I broke them all, threw them all away. What were these paltry things compared to Birchwood, out of whose weeping walls I could knock the bright reverberations of fantasy? I could hide in the hollow sarcophagus of the bench seat on the first landing and peer through a knothole at my family's legs carrying them up and down their day, oblivious of the silent spy who so often in his fancy sent them plunging down the stairs, roaring and flailing, and it was not until many years later, lying under the sacks on the cart while Silas and the rest stamped about outside, that I savoured again the peculiar secret delight of not being found simply because no one realised that I was there to be found. Or I would climb to the attic, where the floor was spread with copper-coloured shallots set to dry, where I once conducted a disturbing and exciting surgical operation on a large female rag doll, and where Mama saw the black shape of her madness coming to claim her. My childhood is gone forever.

On Granny Godkin's last birthday I discovered, obliquely, that I would inherit Birchwood. The old woman's day was a celebration not of longevity but of spite, for she was incredibly old, and the unspoken though general opinion was that if she had any sense of decency she would be dead, and lived on only despite us. My father in his cups was often heard to wonder in an apprehensive undertone if she was after all immortal, and my grandfather, her junior by some years, regarded her across the chasm of silence that separated them with the grudging air of one who suspects he is being cheated.

To say that the house was feverish with activity all day would be an exaggeration, but not a very great one, considering the indolent standards which normally prevailed at Birchwood. Mama worried, of course, and therefore fussed. Since she did not understand why the Godkins fought so much, there was nothing she could to do prevent a row, and therefore determined that at least those arrangements she could affect would be impeccable, and Josie, in the kitchen, turned to her saucepans to hide her wry silent laughter when her distraught mistress threw open the door and cried, as if in answer so some unspoken protest,

'Do it right, Josie, *do it right!*'

My father absented himself for most of the day by paying one of his mysterious and frequent visits to the city. It was said that he kept a woman there, or even women, but that cannot have been true, since the income from the farm was hardly enough to keep the family, never mind a harem. What Mama thought of his jaunts I do not know, but that evening, as the dinner hour drew perilously near, and she came in from the darkening garden with dripping hair and her arms full of wet copper chrysanthemums for the table, she paused, or should I say faltered, to look from the open door down the deserted drive, and her smile was bravely sad as she lied,

'I think I see your Papa coming, do I?'

I went with her into the dining room and leaned on the table while she arranged the flowers in the bowl. Granda Godkin hovered guiltily by the rosewood cabinet in the corner, shuffling his feet, wheezing and sighing, nervously patting the pockets of his jacket. The chrysanthemums glowed in the gloom like living things, gathering to themselves the last light of evening. They seemed to sing, these glorious bright blooms, and I could not take my eyes away from them. When I search in the past it is in moments such as this that I find myself as I was then, an intense little boy standing with his ankles crossed and one arm laid along the table supporting his inclined head, gazing solemnly into the luminous celeste of a dream, or walking gravely, stiff-legged out of the room, stopping as Granda Godkin giggled furtively, and looking back to see Mama turn to the old man slowly with her great sorrowful eyes and softly wail,

'Simon! You've been *drinking*!'

My grandmother had dressed for the occasion in a black bombasine evening gown bedecked with feathers. She wobbled into the dining room on high-heeled black button boots, and Granda Godkin put a hand over his face and peeped at her from between his fingers, quivering with suppressed merriment. The old woman glanced at him and said to Mama, not without a certain grim satisfaction,

'In the rats again, I see.'

She took her place at the head of the table, where I was allowed to approach her, have my cheek kissed, and give her my present, a painting done by me of a crimson horse with three blue legs. She held my head in her arms and rocked back and forth on the chair, making an odd choked cooing little noise, like a rusty hinge. I disengaged myself distastefully and turned to go. Mama prodded me in the small of the back. I was supposed to sing *Happy Birthday*, but having endured the indignity of that embrace I was damned if she was going to get music out of me too. I ran away.

I was curled up on the window seat on the landing, with my arms around my knees, watching the quicksilver rain slide across the black glass, when Papa returned. I looked down through the banisters to the dark hall in time to see his foreshortened figure crash into a chair and send it spinning, and hear his fiercely whispered *Jesus!* Mama slipped out of the dining room, casting a nervous glance behind her before closing the door.

'Are you all right?'

He stood swaying on one leg, rubbing his knee, and did not answer her.

'Are you— ?'

'I'm grand, grand!' He edged around her to the door, but she plucked at his sleeve and whispered urgently into his ear. He shook his head irritably. 'Not a drop, I tell you!'

They went through the door, and I crept downstairs. Josie came forward from the shadows bearing a noisome tray of food, and bent and applied her ear to the keyhole and gave me a con-spiratorial wink.

'Ructions!' she whispered gleefully. Josie derived much bleak amusement from my family's doings. She had been with us for years. Her name was Cotter. They said she had a husband somewhere. She pushed open the door with her foot and entered. Framed by the doorway, the table and the celebrants floated in a little haven of candlelight. Mama sat facing the fireplace with her back turned to me. Granda Godkin's left eye suddenly sprang at me with alarming vacancy over her shoulder. Of my grandmother I could only see her disembodied sharp little face suspended over her plate. Papa stood by the table with one hand in his pocket and the other holding a glass which winked out of a dozen gold and amber eyes. Josie piled food on their plates. Granny Godkin peered suspiciously at her portion and said,

'It doesn't trouble your conscience, I suppose, Joseph, that it's not yours to sell?—Is this supposed to be *chicken*?' She lifted her eyes and glared balefully at Papa. 'I say it's not yours to sell!'

Papa grinned.

'*Not yet*,' he said cheerfully.

Granny Godkin threw up her hands in horror, and turned to Mama. 'O! O! Beatrice, do you hear, he's wishing his own father dead!'

Mama said nothing, but let fall an abrupt lugubrious sob and clapped a hand over her mouth, bowing her head. Josie took up the empty tray. My father finished his drink and sauntered away into the shadows. Granda Godkin farted softly. All these, my loved ones. The pale radiance of the candlelight seemed to invest them with a morose yet passionate vividness, to intensify them, and they became for me, suddenly, creatures with a separate life, who would continue to exist even when I was not there to imagine them, and I recognised, perhaps for the first time, the remote, immutable and persistent nature of the love I wasted on them, as if I had love to waste. Granny Godkin, grinding her jaws in a prelude to another sortie, pointed a chicken leg accusingly at my invisible father, Mama lifted her head and blotted out Granda's glazed staring eye, and then, ah and then, Josie shut the door on them, locking from my sight this new mythology.

I went to bed filled with a vague excitement, conscious that a new mysterious eminence had arisen in my life. *Not yet*. Though I understood nothing, those two words which Papa spoke so carelessly flashed in my mind like gleaming knives which even he could not blunt when, very late that night, he came into my room and stood above the bed in the darkness, breathing heavily and swaying on his feet, and stared at what he took to be his sleeping son and whispered,

'*Who owns you, boy, whose are you, eh?*'

SO BIRCHWOOD was to be mine, that much I understood, albeit dimly. What I failed to see was the plot to deprive me of my inheritance. Aunt Martha was the instigator and prime conspirator. She arrived one bright windy morning in June. There was a rap upon the door, and expectant whispering outside, and then she was in the hall, hallooing her presence, straightening her son's carroty hair, tipping Nockter for having carried in the bags, all at the same time, all the time talking. She was a small intense young woman, quick as a bird, with short red hair and a pale, pointed face. Mama peered apprehensively out of the drawing room, and Aunt Martha let her coat fall to the floor and clapped her little hands.

'*Beatrice !*'

'Martha...O.'

They made a rush at each other, and smacked together in an awkward embrace. Nockter twirled his cap in his fingers and backed out of the hall, and Aunt Martha turned away from her sister-in-law and alighted on me with a tiny cry.

'And this must be Gabriel! My, but isn't he a fine big man? We're going to be great friends, aren't we, Gabriel?'

We were not. I stood stiff and silent as she hugged me, bending away from her aromatic bosom. 'His father's boy,' she said gaily, and releasing me without further ceremony, she reached out a fumbling hand behind her and caught hold of her son. 'This is Michael, also a son of his father, god forgive us. Say how do you do—and try not to dribble, dear.'

He was an odd-looking fellow, small and frail, with sly bright eyes and a fearsome set of teeth. I could see in him nothing of his mother except for his incongruously delicate skin, pale and perfect alabaster, translucent almost. He shuffled his feet while those eyes under their straw-coloured lashes avoided ours, and Aunt Martha, considering him glumly, said,

'My little crucifixion.'

Mama smiled timidly at the boy.

'Poor child,' she murmured. He glanced at her quickly, sharply, and lowered his gaze again. Aunt Martha gave a great squawk of laughter.

'O Beatrice, as soft as ever...' She stopped, and stared past us toward the stairs, at the head of which my father was standing. He was in shirt sleeves, collarless, with hair unkempt, wearing half a beard of lather, staring stonily back into his sister's stare.

'Hello, dear brother,' she said softly, with what I was to come to call her cat-smile, it was so coldly calculating. He did not answer, but merely stood and looked, with one eyebrow quivering, and then went back into the bathroom. The hall was very still, waiting on Aunt Martha. Her eyes were slits, and something peculiar had happened to her mouth. She felt us watching her, and shrugged and turned again to Mama with a bright smile. 'Trissy, tell me all the news, I must hear all the news! Are you still the only sane one in this madhouse?' Mama blushed, and glanced nervously up the stairs. Aunt Martha laid a hand on her arm. 'Don't worry about him, I don't mind, really, I'm used to it by now.'

It was not my father who worried Mama, but Granny Godkin. The time had come and gone for her morning tea and still her curtains had not been drawn. The choice now was to leave her there to work herself into a temper, or bring her down to greet her long-lost daughter. What a choice! We went into the drawing room.

The women sat down by the fire, and Aunt Martha immediately launched into a cheerful account of her trials and troubles. I paid no attention to her tedious rigmarole. Michael and I stood before the window, locked in a tingling silence, and frowned out at the garden where a pair of sparrows were fighting like frantic mechanical toys. A silent scream of boredom began to rise within me, but there rose also a vague fear, vague sense of being threatened by the arrival of this virago and her cretin. No, that is not true.

Only hindsight has endowed me with such a keen nose for nuance. I glanced at the boy by my side. He was no longer watching the garden, for something new was happening behind us, and I had barely time to notice the hush that had descended on the room before there came a kind of strangled wail, and slowly, hardly able to believe our luck, we turned to the fire. Aunt Martha was biting her knuckles and weeping, crouched piteously in her chair with her head bowed. Mama stood over her patting her shoulder and making incoherent little noises meant to comfort, and Michael and I, holding our breath, took one cautious step forward and gazed blissfully upon the immensely satisfying spectacle of a grown-up dissolving in a puddle of grief.

Of all our histories, Aunt Martha's is perhaps the most bizarre. She was the black sheep of the Godkins, if such a term means anything when speaking of my family. In the town she was known as a brazen hussy from the time she was a child, and was once, I believe, denounced from the popish pulpit in a veiled though obvious reference to bad companions. However, it was not until a certain summer of her young womanhood that she gave the gossips some real red meat on which to chew, and she was hardly sure of her own condition before the town also knew, in that mysterious way towns have of knowing such things, that she was expecting a little surprise. All hell broke loose in the happy house of Birchwood. Granny Godkin beat her daughter about the head with a silver-backed hairbrush. Papa returned from his honeymoon.

For nine long months Martha was not allowed outside the grounds. She spent her time wandering in the wood, or sitting by the lake, with a sly secret smile in her eyes, hatching her plot. Her firstborn arrived that spring day of storm and panic when the circus invaded Birchwood, and Papa, dismounting that evening by the fountain, looked up and saw an infant lifted in the window. However, that infant was I, but more of that presently. Aunt Martha had already prepared for her departure. She paused only long enough to confer with Papa behind locked doors, and then bundled up her son and took flight. Granny Godkin stayed in bed for a week.

And Martha's mysterious lover? Rumour had an inspired farrago of a story, according to which the leader of the Magic Circus, the travelling troupe of shams which had laid siege to our house, one Prospero by name, a magician apparently, had with Aunt Martha's enthusiastic cooperation conjured up the makings of that homunculus that stood beside me now gaping at its mother. I cannot say where rumour found evidence to support its claims, but the story had one point in its favour, that is, it held that the invasion by the circus was nothing more, or less, than Prospero's effort to claim his son and heir. Well, I shall say nothing. People must have their myths. Some said that Prospero was a cripple, some that he had a cloven hoof. One story, the favourite, and still current, had him a midget! A few held, however, that the magician did not exist. I shall say nothing.

After Aunt Martha's departure, Granny Godkin had never spoken her name again until, these many years later, a letter arrived to say that the wanton was coming home. Then my grandmother smiled her smile, and wrote a gracious reply, and waited, and now Martha had returned, and she was to tutor me in the sciences and humanities, god help me.

Michael and I stood with our eyes out on stalks and watched that grief bubbling until Mama turned at last and looked at us reproachfully. Her hand, behind her back where Aunt Martha could not see it, indicated the door. Reluctantly, we left the room, and plodded up the stairs with solemn tread, like two grave little old men. This is the landing, a spacious carpeted court, twin to the hall below, with tall gleaming windows affording a view across trees and fields to the quivering pale line of the distant sea. And there is the lake, see it gleam, wind-whipped. Michael said nothing, but paced behind me in silence, turning his eyes obediently where I pointed. Birchwood is a big house, three storeys topped by a warren of attics. We trailed through the empty bedrooms, pausing here before a pockmarked mirror, there by a trunk mysteriously crammed with broken crockery. I showed him the narrow back stairs which crept down surreptitiously, under bald linoleum, to a gloomy subterranean vault wedged between two doors, a rickety one bolted against the creeping green damp of the back yard, and another, panelled with green glass, opening on a potted palm and three deep steps which led, presto!, into the front hall. We examined the muddy paintings in the library, the bust of an unidentified blind Greek, the complicated affair of rods and knobs by which the french windows

35

were locked. Josie was on her hands and knees under the dining-room table, motionless, staring at nothing. We stood in the door-way and looked at her, and then retired silently. Aunt Martha was still weeping by the drawing-room fire. Mama glared at us. We climbed the stairs again.

In my room, Michael sat on the bed with his hands dangling between his bony knees while I laid out my toys for his delectation in an arc before him on the floor. We stared at them as we had stared at everything else, speechless and bored. In my imagination I was standing haughtily over him, with a hand resting elegantly on my hip, telling him just how things were, blockhead, this is my house, and these are my toys, so don't get any ideas, see?

'You have a lot of things,' he said, with a faint, faintly mocking smile, though whether it was me or himself that he mocked I could not tell, though I can now.

My most precious toy, if that is the right word, was a magnificent circular jigsaw puzzle of over two thousand tiny wafer-thin pieces. After weeks of intermittent labour varying between a furious panicstricken scrabbling and the smiling swoon of delight when the right piece, the only possible piece, fell into its place in the mosaic, I had assembled out of it a glorious gold and blue painting of a Renaissance madonna, a picture which, in the completed puzzle, glowed with a sense of light and purity, of palpable intensity, which was mysteriously absent from its sibling reproduced on the lid of its box. This tormentor now lay docile at Michael's feet, where he examined it with uncertain sidelong glances. Abruptly, before I could stop him, he bent and picked up the board. Horrified, I tried to snatch it from him, it tilted, and the puzzle glided off, seemed to hang intact in mid-air for a moment, and then fell to the carpet and shattered with an absurdly inadequate, heartbreaking little clatter. Michael stared at the pieces, his mouth moving silently. Any colour there was in his face faded, leaving it a bonewhite mask of fury. The intensity of this speechless rage frightened me. I looked again at the shattered thing, and I could have wept. *Cretin!* It was not the wasted work that pained me, but the unavoidable recognition of the fragility of all that beauty. I turned without a word and stalked out of the room.

I sat down on the highest step of the stairs, my favourite place to sulk, and was in time to see Granny Godkin hobble into the drawing room. The house rang with angry voices, the slamming of doors, heavy footfalls. Godkin fights were always dispersed, mobile affairs that sprawled across two or three rooms simultaneously. Michael came and sat down quietly by my side. I ignored him. Downstairs, the drawing-room door flew open and my father strode out, halted, looked up at us without seeing us, and turned back in the doorway and shouted,

'*No!*'

He plunged across the hall into the library, and a moment later an unseen hand gently closed the drawing-room door. Michael cleared his throat.

'Ever see juggling?' he asked.

I disdained to answer. Granda Godkin came out of the dining room and, stealthily, his ear turned toward the drawing room, tiptoed after Papa into the library, only to come flying out again immediately and flee to the back of the house. Michael took from his pocket a chipped blue building block, a marble and a rubber ball. He began to juggle. At first it went clumsily, he dropped the ball, hit himself on the nose with the block, but then all abruptly changed, a rhythm appeared, one could almost hear it, like the airy beat of a bird's wing, and in his hands he spun a trembling pale blue hoop of light. His uplifted face gleamed from the effort of concentration as he leaned this way and that, following a sudden dip of the block, the wayward flight of the ball, and I found myself thinking of air and angels, of silence, of translucent planes of pale blue glass in space gliding through illusory, gleaming and perfect combinations. My puzzle seemed a paltry thing compared to this beauty, this, this *harmony*. The drawing-room door opened again and Mama led out Aunt Martha, sobbing and snuffling. Michael, his concentration shattered, dropped the ball. It descended the stairs in three high hops and skidded between the women's feet. Michael laughed, an odd noise, rose, dropped forward on all fours, gave a little kick, and stood on his hands. Like that, legs waving, teeth clenched in an inverted grin, he walked down the steps. I think I cheered. Aunt Martha lifted her head to find this grotesque thing advancing slowly toward her, and she opened her mouth and gave a shriek of mingled fright and woe. Mama put an arm around her shoulders and took her into the dining room.

Michael retrieved the ball, stood upright, and came slowly

back up the stairs, wiping the sweat from his forehead. He stopped below me and leaned against the banisters, tossing the ball from hand to hand. We were silent for a moment, and then he said,

'She's always crying.' He waited for me to reply. I could think of nothing to say. We considered the ceiling. He sighed. 'She gives me a pain.'

We tittered. He sat down beside me and handed me the ball.

'Hard to juggle with, a ball,' he said. 'Too light.'

I agreed.

I HAD EXPECTED, perhaps even hoped, that their arrival would immediately transform life at Birchwood. Nothing is so simple. Things changed, certainly, but slowly, and in subtle ways. The morning rituals, the fights, the elaborate, barely edible evening dinners, they remained unaltered, but the patterns woven by these set-dances of life shifted gradually, until the whole mesh of emphasis and echo between the inhabitants of the house was warped. New alliances were struck. Granny Godkin astonished us all that first morning when, having risen at an unprecedented late hour, she embraced her tear-stained daughter before the drawing-room fire and spoke to her kindly, even lovingly. They closeted themselves in the old woman's room and were not seen again until that evening, when my grandfather was allowed into the sanctum, another precedent, in my time at least. Later he was led out in a flood of maudlin tears. Mama seemed uncertain whether all this lovingkindness relieved or disquieted her, but she smiled as always, and believed the best of people, as always. My father stalked softly about the house wearing a scowl of profound suspicion. Nothing is simple.

My schooling began almost immediately. By any other standards than my own, Aunt Martha was a dreadful teacher, but by mine she was ideal. She was blissfully ignorant of those subjects which a little boy is supposed to study, and I sometimes wondered if she was aware that such esoteric things as Latin, or vulgar fractions, existed in any sense that could apply to her young charge. To Aunt Martha, education was simply a synonym for books, any and all books, and since what one read was irrelevant so long as one did read, the selection was entirely arbitrary. After all, I could not know everything, so what did it matter which parts of the great sum of knowledge I approached? The only imprimatur a subject required was her ignorance of it, and the scope of her ignorance was impressive. For instance, she was convinced that if one sailed steadily westward along the equator one would, without ever touching dry land, astonish the point from which one had departed by sneaking up on it from behind eighty days later, or perhaps it was seventy-nine, one had to reckon with something called the dateline. Verne, therefore, with the help of Columbus and Marco Polo, taught me my befogged geography, not its facts but its poetry, for they delineated not meridians and poles, but a glorious chart of dreams. Ferdinand and Isabella sailed a bright balloon in search of Cathay, that fabulous rumour in the east, and I followed them on my paper wings.

I did not like Aunt Martha, she was a hard woman to like, but, having been ignored all my short life by all the family save Mama, who ignored me in her own way by treating me as an extension of herself, the fact that my aunt would devote three hours of her day solely to me was, shall I say flattering? Directly breakfast was over on the day after her arrival she announced briskly that she was ready to begin the great task. The announcement was greeted by a weary silence, and when she tried again, in case we had not heard the first time, Papa showed his teeth in a smile and inquired with ominous sweetness if we might be allowed to digest the bloody breakfast before she started giving orders. At that she threw down her napkin, the unmistakeable battle signal of the Godkins, but Mama jumped up and said of course, of course, the sooner the better, no time to lose, the child was backward enough as it was, and she whisked Aunt Martha and me up to the schoolroom.

This was a damp gloomy place at the top of the house, a relic of that lost age when the women of Birchwood bore whole battalions of children avid for knowledge. There were a dozen little desks ranged in three neat rows of four facing a delicately-made spindly lectern, curiously reminiscent of the ideal of a Victorian governess for whose service it had been built. Behind the lectern there was a large triangular window, silvered with rain now but which on bright days offered a cruelly enticing view across fields to the beach and the gay blue sea. Long blackboards ran the length of both walls to right and left of the desks, one of them set higher than the other owing to the slope of the ceiling. This imbalance added an incongruously jaunty touch to the sober oakbrown atmosphere of the room. Josie and her erratic duster had been there before us, but the legs of the lectern were still draped with an intricate filigree of cobwebs.

'This is grand,' Aunt Martha said dubiously. The place seemed fitted for a sterner sense of duty than hers. Mama, smiling, nodding encouragement, backed out of the room and softly closed the door. I sat down at one of the desks. How cold and smooth was the wood. The rain drummed on the window, a melancholy whisper. Aunt Martha stood and stared out of unfocused eyes, with that expression of quiet baffled despair which always seemed to take hold of the faces of grown-ups when their thoughts forgot themselves. I drew invisible patterns on the desk with a fingertip. The squeak of my nail on the wood recalled her from her brooding. She went and crouched over the ancient oilstove in the corner, chafing her hands and muttering under her breath. With her imitation smile she turned to me.

'Well Gabriel, what do you know and not know? What would you like to learn?'

Nothing. Mama had taught me to read, in a perfunctory kind of way, and of course I knew my prayers off by rote, but apart from these graces I was a small, well-behaved savage. I wonder if I have changed, even yet? I have forgotten my prayers, that is something. Aunt Martha's bright smile quailed before my silence, and she wandered off about the room, searching fretfully for something that might interest me. She pushed open a sliding wooden panel in the wall and found a sunken bookcase.

'Ah, now this is what we need. Let's see, how about—poo! this dust. I suppose you've read all these already, have you? No? Well, we'll see if we can find something exciting, something really...'

I stopped listening, and cautiously opened the lid of the desk. Inside I found a blunt pencil, a jotter with curled yellow leaves, and a hard shrunken brown thing like a nut, which on closer inspection turned out to be an ancient apple core. Who had left these relics here for me to find? My imagination failed against such a mystery. Dead, all dead. My spine tingled. Aunt Martha at last chose a book, and pushed the desk beside me close to mine. She sat down. The book was called *The Something Twins*, something like that, I barely glanced at it. She began to read, and I put a hand under my chin and considered the window, thinking what a glorious pleasure it would be to smash each of those pearly panes. Only a child knows· what it is to be truly bored. *Gabriel and Rose lived in a big house by the sea. One day, when she was very young, little Rose disappeared, and Gabriel went away in search of her...*Crash went the glass, and daggers of crystal dropped down and stabbed Josie in the back of the neck as she came out into the yard below to feed the chickens. What fun! Slowly I became aware that the voice at my ear had fallen silent. Gabriel? Rose? *Rose?* Aunt Martha sat with the book open on one hand, one finger pressed to her cheek, her face turned toward me, watching me attentively. I had the eerie notion that she was listening to the ticking of my thoughts. She hummed a short snatch of a tune under her breath and then said,

'Do you never miss—? but of course you wouldn't, you couldn't have known...' She laughed shrilly. She seemed nervous. Her fingers danced by themselves on the desk. 'How silly I am! Aren't I silly, Gabriel? Tell me, tell me this, would you like a little sister to play with, hmm?' Suddenly, to my disgust and intense discomfort, she swept me into her arms. The book tumbled to the floor. 'You poor child,' she whispered, her breath flowing down my cheek like warm syrup. 'You poor poor child!' She thrust me away from her with that hearty husky tenderness at which she was adept, and, holding me at arm's length, gazed upon me with brimming eyes. 'Your Mama says you never cry...?'

I stared fixedly past her shoulder and squirmed slowly, cautiously, out of her clutches. So we sat for a moment, panting softly. It was all so very odd. I felt that some vital and strange event had taken place without my noticing. Aunt Martha suddenly smiled her sly smile, looking inexplicably triumphant. She picked up the book from the floor.

'Gabriel and Rose...'

Her voice followed me down two flights of stairs before it faded. At the door of the library Mama met me with a look of alarm.

'Where are you off to? Has Aunt Martha...? Gabriel? What are you doing?'

On a little low table by the bookshelves there was a small framed photograph of a young girl in white standing among leaves in a garden, leaning out of the tree's deep shade into a mist of sunlight. In one hand she held a flower. A rose. Look!

THE MAIN REASON I was not sent away to a proper school was that we could not afford it. The finances of Birchwood were dwindling at the same rate as the decline of Papa's interest in the farm, which had never been great anyway. I can still see him, with ink-stained fingers and collar agape, his gold tooth glittering, crouched at his desk in the library in a pool of lamplight, scrabbling desperately among a litter of bills, and, a little later, standing in the shadows, where glass clinked furtively on glass, running his fingers through his hair, soothing himself. Of course our genteel slide toward penury was never mentioned, not in my presence, but the silent evidence of it was everywhere around me, in the cracked paint and the missing tiles, the dry rot that ate its way unchecked across the floors and up the stairs, in the games of musical chairs which Mama played, switching them from the front rooms to the back in a circle of increasing degeneracy until the day when, groaning and creaking, they regained their original places and the wheel ceased to turn. A leak, preceded by a burgeoning grey patch of damp, appeared in the schoolroom ceiling. Nockter, after an inspection of the roof, reported that half the slates had come loose and some were gone altogether. It would be repaired within days, Papa promised, he would get a man out from town, but the days became weeks, and I studied to the intricate accompaniment of the plop and splash of rainwater falling into a battery of jamjars ranged around me, and at last Aunt Martha and I were forced to abandon the schoolroom for the library. Then an army of rats laid siege to the kitchen.

The final proof, the clincher, as they say, that the Godkins were going the way of all the gentry, that is down, was the newfound boldness of the peasants. As my people knew, and lucky they did, there is nothing that will keep the Irish in their place like a well-appointed mansion. They may despise and hate you, only put a fine big house with plenty of windows in it up on a hill and bejapers you have them be the balls, stunned into a cringing, cap-touching coma. But beware. It is a fragile thraldom. The first unmended fence will mean the first snigger behind your back outside the chapel yard, an overrun garden will bring them grinning to the gate, and a roof left in visible disrepair will see them poaching your land in daylight, as now they poached ours, contemptuous not only of the law but even of my father's shotgun, which was no mean threat. That summer he took to rising early, long before dawn, to stalk the wood in search of the wolves who were decimating his flock. Often I was woken by his stealthy preparations, the creak of his boots on the stairs, the muffled rattle of cartridges, that abrupt crisp click as he broke the gun over his arm, and in my warm world under the blankets these sounds expressed exactly what I thought to be the control, the heroism and the humour of his venture. The side door closed softly behind him, and the silence reorganised itself to await his return. I imagined him moving through the chill black morning, across the lawn, slipping into the wood so quietly that it hardly noticed him, and then he was no longer what I knew, but was become an element of air and darkness, of leaves, thrilling and strange, an icy grin burning under the still trees.

Sometimes his safaris produced a trophy, and he might appear at first light with a crofter's wild-eyed son by the scruff of the neck and a brace of strangled pheasants over his shoulder, but I never knew him to do anything worse to a poacher than warn him that by god if he ever showed his snout near Birchwood again he would get a backside full of buckshot. Such warnings mostly went unheeded, but then I do not really think Papa wanted it otherwise, for the birds were only important to him now as bait for this subtler game. But I remember one morning early I was awakened by a confused clamour in the wood, shouts and challenges and the sudden grim roar of a shotgun, and I scrambled to the window and saw a little old man with bandy legs and a hat pulled down to his ears come crashing out of the trees into the delicately-lit dawn garden. His neat green footprints in the dewy grass traced a wide arc behind him as he galloped across the lawn toward the corner of the house and the lane he must have known was there which struck off around the tip of the wood to the road and escape. In one hand he clutched a dead pheasant, and in the other some other bird, a woodcock perhaps. Those winged things flapping and fluttering at the ends of his outstretched arms made it seem as if he were trying to take wing himself. He was skidding past the fountain when Papa, hastily slipping a cartridge into the gun, stepped through the gap the old boy had broken in the trees. He fired from the hip. A downstairs window shattered, and someone in the house squealed in sleepy terror. The poacher faltered, and glanced over his shoulder. Ahead of him a figure in a dressing gown appeared around the corner of the house and stood crouched in his path, capering excitedly. It was Granda Godkin. I would swear I heard the clatter of bones as the two old codgers crashed together. The woodcock, resuscitated for one splendid moment, flew straight up between them, shedding a spray of feathers in its wake. The poacher bounced off Granda Godkin, stumbled, regained his balance, drew back his arm and smacked him across the side of the head with the pheasant. More feathers, flying blood. Granda tottered, keeled over on his back, and the poacher sprang across his supine body and disappeared, leaving his hat behind him slowly spinning on the grass. Papa, the gun shaking in his hands, came and glared down at his fallen father, and for one wild moment I thought he was going to shoot him, but instead he turned on his heel and stamped toward the house, pausing only, almost absentmindedly, to release the second barrel of the shotgun into the wood, blasting a ragged hole in the leaves.

'*Shite!*'

When I got downstairs the blood-spattered old man was being deposited on a couch in the drawing room. Mama, half dressed, walked around in circles, speechless and pale. My father gibbered furiously. Aunt Martha cursed him. It was pandemonium. They swabbed the gore on Granda's face and found that most of it was birdblood, though he had the beginnings of a splendid black eye, and the bird, dead and all as it was, had bitten a neat little comma from the rim of his ear. He turned up his eyes until only the whites were visible, or should I say the yellows, and moaned without ceasing. The window which Papa had shot was in splinters, and the wall behind the couch was pockmarked with pellets. He kicked a chair.

'I know his face, I'll get his name, by god I'll make him hop...'
He stopped. Aunt Martha, bent over her father, had turned her
head to glance at Papa with the faintest of smiles. He stared back
at her, eyes popping, his mouth still working, and then suddenly
he laughed, silently, and his shoulders shook. He crept out of the
room. Granda Godkin wailed. He was never to recover from that
dawn adventure.

Poachers were one thing, but more sinister by far were those
other intruders who began to appear, mysterious wanton creatures
glimpsed across the lake, or trailing down the fields toward the
beach, a crowd of them, five or six, moving through the wood at
dusk. The curious thing is that no one spoke of them, although we
all must have seen them, unless I was subject to visions. It was as
if their presence were an embarrassment. They might have been
ghosts had they not been indifferent to the sombre duties of ghost-
hood, for these visitants laughed and chattered, they were almost
boisterous, but also, when I think of it, there was a certain distant
quality about them, an aloofness, which had nothing to do with
either ghostliness or the fact that they were seen only from a
distance. They were like people at the far end of a room bent in
unheard laughter whose private joke invests them with an impenetrable self-possession. It seemed impossible that they feared god
or man, and perhaps it was their lack of fear which frightened
us, for indeed we were afraid of them. My father's eyes began to
display an edgy rear-regardant look, like that of a man pursued by
playful furies, and often Mama would fall abruptly silent in the
middle of a sentence and stare through the window toward the
murmurous wood.

I think it was Michael and I who saw them first, one gloomy
evening down near Cotter's place where we had built a fire. Our
uneasy relationship had progressed with painful slowness through
silences that were like endurance tests, and brief awkward disclosures which left us embarrassed and weary. I tried to interest
him in the fantastical possibilities of the house, but he only smiled
his enigmatic smile and moved away from me. Even then, in
spite of our shared birthday, he was older than I. He had never
learned to live indoors. I often came upon him standing stock still
on one foot in the middle of a room, speechless and agonised,
staring with that white fury at the shattered bits of an ashtray
or a vase at his feet. He was obsessed by fire and water, by hawks

and other wild things, and although Aunt Martha had excluded him from our lessons only to humiliate him, for she made a great show of despising her son, he seemed perfectly happy to forgo the joys of learning, and went to work on the farm instead. O but he was no bumpkin, no. He worked at farming, and hunted with Nockter, drank porter in secret, ate with his hands, but behind his rough ways there was something hard and cold and clever. He was playing a part, you see, just like the rest of us, only sometimes he betrayed the icy amusement, the steely anger, the pain, those things which made him a Godkin. I cannot say that I ever liked him, but there was between us a bond which would not be ignored however we tried, and we did try. Hence the silences, the disclosures, the sudden charges we made at each other across the distance that separated us, only to be jerked back by our congenital coldness from the final contact, that squelchy slap a human creature experiences when it surrenders to another.

He had attended school for a while and the religious instruction he had suffered there at the hands of the nuns formed the basis of many of our first conversations. In a house where religion was regarded, like foxhunting, as nothing more than a ritual proof of the indestructibility of our class, my own initiation into the celestial mysteries had been sketchy, to say the least, and I was not prepared for the rigour and savagery of that cult whose implacable paradoxes the good nuns had expounded to Michael. That day down in the crippled wood, while we sat like frogs by the fire with our ears buried in our collars, he told me about hell. It appears that if we follow the dictates of the nature god has given us, our reward will be to fry eternally in a lovingly prepared oven, whereas if we persist in denying the undeniable truth about ourselves we will be allowed to float for all time through an empty blue immensity, the adoration of the lord our only task. A most extraordinary concept, which we found screamingly funny, though we acknowledged the humour of it only by thoughtful sighs and gloomy silences, which is how children laugh at the vagaries of adults.

'Just think of it,' he mused, gazing into the singing flames. 'Roasting. That would be awful. I remember a priest came once to give a mission, for three days, you know, praying and so on. He had a cross in his belt and he kept fiddling with it, I remember that, pulling at it. He said that if we did things to ourselves we'd be put into a special part of hell. I suppose he meant we'd have devils sticking forks in our mickeys. He was funny.' He paused, and poked at the embers with a charred twig, faintly smiling. 'Do you know what I did? After school I had to burn the dustbins, out behind the camp.' He sniggered. 'I did it into the fire!'

Did what? I laughed uncertainly, wondering what he could mean. Some happy thought struck him and he laughed again.

'*I nearly put the fire out.*'

Then I heard them. They were above us. I heard their low voices, soft laughter, the crunch of dry leaves under their feet, and soon they appeared, flickering through the trees, a fat man and a fatter woman, a tall thin figure in a black coat, two girls and a youth, a small boy. Michael had not taken his eyes from the fire. I tugged at his sleeve, and he turned, unhappily, irritably, and snapped,

'What do you want?'

I shrugged, obscurely angry at him, and looked up again and watched the crowd climb the hill diagonally and disappear over the ridge into the birch wood. I was not frightened, not exactly, but I felt a mingled excitement and dread, and a sensation of controlled and not unpleasant panic. I turned to Michael again, silently questioning. He glanced at me, away, nonchalant.

'What's up? Did you see something? The fire's going out.'

I stared at him. Why should he lie?

THEY SEWED UP Granda Godkin's ear and bathed his black eye back to its former jaundiced shade, but they could do nothing for his maimed brain. Now he shuffled between the poles of his existence, the dining room, the lavatory, his bed, wrapped in a numbed impenetrable lethargy, crouching under imaginary blows. Sometimes he would disappear for hours, to be discovered at last in a shuttered room standing bolt upright with his back pressed to the wall and his stricken wide eyes glowing faintly in the gloom. These periods of catalepsy terrified Mama. In her first year at Birchwood he had thrown, if that is the word, two epileptic fits, and although she had not witnessed them she was convinced that one day he would fling himself down at her feet, snapping and foaming, to expire slowly, with a great clamour of rattling heels and gnashing teeth, while she stood over him helplessly, gazing back horrified into his numbed beseeching eyes. Doc McCabe had once warned her that the old man must never be allowed alcohol. Now she fitted a rusty padlock on the rosewood cabinet in the dining room, and, sure that she had hit on a cure, walked out into the hall and found Granda Godkin teetering on the stairs, knees bent and arms outstretched, his fingers twitching, emitting through clenched teeth a high-pitched birdlike screech, and she was forced to admit finally that his mind was forever frozen in that moment of collision and clatter, feathers and blood, when that furious winged great creature had flung itself upon him in the dawning garden.

He ventured less and less often out of his room, and then took to his bed permanently. I was made to sit with him, I suppose on the principle that an old man should want the youngest carrier of his name and seed near him at the end. I suspect Granda Godkin could have managed without me. These vigils were excruciating. He lay motionless, watching his hands on the counterpane with profound suspicion, as though convinced that *they* had slipped into the bed an immensely patient, crafty assassin who was only waiting for a chance to throttle him. I sat on a hard chair trying to remain absolutely still, for at the slightest movement his lizard eyes flickered venomously at me. The air in the darkened room was viscous, tainted with faint odours, wax and excrement. My indifference toward the old boy turned to hatred. I wondered where his thoughts could possibly be during all those long days of immobility and silence. Old men have their interests, collecting stamps, antique matchboxes, interfering with little girls, but the most I could recall of his life was a wicked grin shuffling down the hall and a face staring vacantly into a fire. He had wasted that wealth of days, scooped out and discarded their hearts, happiest with husks. So much emptiness appalled me, I tried to creep away, those yellow eyes transpierced me.

One morning there was a startling change in his condition. Mama found him sitting up in bed rubbing his hands gleefully, trembling with excitement. God had come to visit him in the night.

'That's nice,' said Mama. 'Did he have anything to say?'

He gave her a crafty sidelong look, became suddenly morose, and changed the subject by petulantly demanding his false teeth. They had been in a little glass there beside the bed. Where were they gone? She tried to outmanoeuvre him.

'You know, I'm sure Mr Culleton would be very interested to hear about—'

'Bugger that—where's my teeth?'

She had taken away that dangerous set of weapons while he slept. Now she brought them back. Poor Mama, no tenacity.

'Where's Joseph?' he cried, clacking his choppers. 'I want to talk to Joseph.'

But when my father was found the old man had forgotten what he wanted to say. He lapsed again into silence and staring. By the afternoon he was delirious. An enormous woodlouse, he told us, was lumbering around the room with elephantine tread, blind antennae feeling the fetid air, searching for him. The louse, it seems, was god come a second time. The old man tried to flee from his bed and had to be restrained by force. His withered frame hid unexpected reserves of strength. The vicar and the doctor arrived together, unlikely angels of death. The Reverend Culleton had five minutes alone with the fast-failing sinner and came out of the sickroom looking decidedly shaken. Doc McCabe, hardly less decrepit than his patient, just looked down at the old man and shook his head.

'*What's wrong with him?*' Papa whispered. The whole business of this dying had come smack in the middle of a delicate and complex land deal.

'Poor Simon,' the Doc sighed. 'Dear me, it seems like only yesterday...'

'Yes yes, but what's *wrong* with him?'

'For god's sake man, it's a wonder he's alive at all! He's as strong as a horse, must be.' Papa looked down doubtfully at the ancient foetus in the bed. McCabe suddenly cackled. 'It wouldn't surprise me if he lived another couple of years!'

Papa slowly closed his eyes.

'Christ,' he muttered, and walked away.

Granny Godkin refused to acknowledge that her sometime husband was on the way out. Perhaps she did not want to be reminded of her own approaching extinction, or maybe she was just not interested in the old man's going. I favour the latter. She sat by the fire in the drawing room all day and greeted Aunt Martha's bulletins from the sickroom with a deaf smile.

'What's that you say, my dear...?'

I was summoned to the bedside in the evening. Granda Godkin wished to say goodbye to me. For a long time he said nothing. The others, at my back, began to fidget. He gazed through me, into his private pale blue eternity, and it was as if he were already dead, a mere memory, he was so thin and faded. At last his eyes came back and focused on me. He took me for my father, and said very clearly,

'Joe, you'll never be anything but a waster!'

That was his farewell. I knew that those attendant silences behind me expected something of me, but what it was I did not know. I tried to take his hand but he would not let me lift it, and turned his face to the wall, so I caught hold of one of his brown-paper fingers and shook it solemnly and then made my escape. Did I mourn him? I suppose I did, in my way. But I felt, as I have felt at every death, that something intangible had slipped through my fingers before I discovered its nature. All deaths are scandalously mistimed. People do not live long enough. They come and go, briefly, shadows dwindling toward an empty blue noon.

One memory, hardly worth mentioning, but here it is, for lack of something finer. He taught me to ride a bicycle. In spring it was, of course, an April evening, sunlight, wind in the trees, the crocuses sprouting. A dog followed us, a miserable creature with a swollen belly and moist eyes. Granda Godkin loathed animals, he picked fights with them. That evening he would stop suddenly, turn, stamp his foot, growl. The tyke stopped too, looked at him attentively, one ear quivering, and set off after us again. The old man held the back of the saddle and trotted beside me, wheezing and gasping, roaring encouragement. I sat perched on this impossibly spindly, wobbling contraption with my heart in my mouth, pedalling furiously and getting nowhere until Granda, with one last tremendous shove, let go his hold and sent me sailing on alone. The handlebars trembled, the front wheel hit a stone, I squealed in fright, and then I felt a kind of *click*, I cannot describe it, and the bike was suddenly transformed into a fine and delicate instrument as light as air. The taut spokes sang. I flew! That gentle rising against the evening air, that smooth flow onwards into the blue, it is as near as earthbound creatures ever come to flying. It did not last long, I jumped down awkwardly, landed on my crotch on the crossbar, and the back wheel ran over my foot. I turned and looked back at Granda Godkin, shuffling behind me. He was speaking. Congratulations, surely?

'I'm after twisting me hip!' he cried.

He lived until late in the night, when I was awakened not by a sound but by something in the silence going awry. There was someone in the corridor. I peeped out. A shimmering pale figure descended the stairs swiftly and disappeared from view. The front door opened, I heard it, and felt the faint night air. A gleam of light fell across the landing and was immediately extinguished. The air bore traces of a woody perfume which at first I could not identify, I think because it was so familiar. There was a soft rustling sound followed by a gasp, and another figure appeared and crawled on hands and knees to the head of the stairs. He slithered down the first few steps, paused, and with a tiny cry

53

plunged on down into the darkness. I was turning back into my room when I heard, far below, a bark like that of an animal in pain, and when I looked out from my window I saw him again, scuttling like a maimed crab across the lawn into the wood where a bird was singing, such beauty, such passion, a nightingale perhaps, although I do not think there are nightingales in this part of the world. Was it near dawn then? I went back to bed. Cigar smoke, yes, yes, wearily, sleepily, I admitted it.

They found him early in the morning in the birch wood, curled like a stillborn infant in the grass. His ruined mouth was open, caked with black blood, and it was not until they were moving him that they discovered, in the tree beside which he lay, his false teeth sunk to the gums like vicious twin pink parasites in the bark. Aunt Martha came to my room to break the news to me. All I could do was sit on the side of the bed, speechless and numb, with my socks in my hand, and stare at her shimmering white nightgown, admitting to myself what I already knew, that I had not been dreaming. Exasperated by my dullness, she caught my shoulders and shook me until my jaws rattled.

'*Do you never cry!*'
Not yet.

WITH GRANDA GODKIN gone at last my father came into his inheritance. On the very day that the will was read, confirming his freedom, Papa sold off fifty acres to old man Gaddern of Halfmile House, who, it was rumoured, was financing the rebels in the area, partly from sympathy but mostly as a means of ensuring the safety of his portion of the new State the revolution would found. Along with other sales made on the sly while my grandfather was still alive, this latest iniquity left Birchwood crippled, with the Gaddern swine crowding us on three sides and the sea at our back. Papa got drunk at dinner that night, and when Granny Godkin launched her inevitable attack on him he just sat back and laughed at her, picking his teeth with a matchstick.

'Times are hard, mother, times are hard. Have another glass of wine.'

'Wine! Your father not cold in his grave and you...you...You were only waiting for him to die. Are you human at all?'

'Aye, unlike yourself, all too human. Show me your glass here, come on.'

The old woman began to blubber, not very convincingly, and turned to Aunt Martha for support. If Papa was Granda Godkin's heir, his sister was being groomed as Granny's. Someone had to carry on the struggle. Martha, looking splendidly menacing in black, went to her mother's side to comfort her.

'You're a pig, Joseph Godkin,' said my aunt. 'You always were.'

He laughed, and banged the table with his fist.

'Beatrice, do you hear? That's the thanks we get for taking her and her brat in off the roads.'

Mama would not lift her head. She said quietly,

'Joe, please, the boys...'

'Ah let them listen, see what they'll be up against when the time comes.' He turned to his sister again and considered her contemptuously. 'By Christ, it's a laugh. The whores are on horseback.'

Aunt Martha grimaced in disgust and would not answer him. Granny Godkin, disappointed I think at her protégé's apparent lack of spirit, pushed her daughter out of the line of fire and cried,

'A goodfornothing drunkard, that's all you are. *And god forgive me that I ever had you.* Now!'

Papa opened his mouth and closed it again, looking slowly from one of us to the other. We avoided his eye. His uncertain gaze distressed us. It was unthinkable that he, the rock on which our fortunes so perilously teetered, should crack under the pressure of a mere family row. Mama's knife clattered as she dropped it on her plate. She blushed. On occasions such as this her greatest wish seemed to be to merge quietly into the wallpaper and disappear. Michael, hunched over his dinner, looked out cautiously at Aunt Martha from under his pale brows. Papa shook his head wearily and crossed with heavy tread to the french windows and drew them open on the still night. From the garden there entered the fragrance of flowers and trees, of earth, a sturdy sensuousness which hovered on the thick tepid air of the room like an uninvited and unwelcome guest. Papa chuckled softly, rocking on his heels.

'We might as well get what we can while we can,' he said softly. 'They're taking over.'

He put his hands into his pockets and sauntered off into the darkness, whistling. Granny Godkin shrugged, and clutched her shawl tightly about her shoulders.

'Drunken nonsense!' she snapped. 'Rubbish. Beatrice! Will you shut that window before I catch my death.'

Mama obediently rose to close out the unsettling night, but suddenly Papa reared up out of the darkness, wild-eyed, his hair on end and his suit smeared with mud, a startling transfiguration. He pushed Mama aside and flung himself at Aunt Martha.

'*You!*' he roared, and thrust a trembling forefinger under her nose. 'You and your whelp can get out if you don't like it here. Nothing to stop you!'

Aunt Martha folded her arms and gazed at him calmly, smiling faintly. His eyes bulged, and two small bright crimson stains appeared on his cheekbones. His tie was twisted under his left ear. I knew, by a sudden unimpeachable intuition, that he had tripped over the bicycle which I had left lying on its side on the lawn, and I had to look into Mama's tormented face to keep myself from laughing.

'*Pig*,' said Aunt Martha, jabbing the word like a needle into Papa's face, and carelessly picked a thread from her sleeve. He reached out behind him to the half-dead wine bottle on the table and flung it across the room. It burst against the wall with an understated plop and sprayed blood-red wine down Michael's back. A curved splinter of pink glass flew up in an arc and splashed into the water jug beside Granny Godkin's plate, and the old woman gave a squeak of fright. Aunt Martha sprang to her feet, ready to howl, but Papa suddenly turned to her with an admonitory finger to his lips. He smiled. She stood aghast, her mouth and eyes wide open, and he took his finger from his lips and waved it roguishly at her and then stalked softly out of the room. I was shocked, not by his violence, that was nothing new, but by something odd and humourously sinister which I had perceived in that balletic moment between them, a moment frozen forever for me in the precise picture of his smile which I retain to this day. Mama stared at her sister-in-law, and through clenched teeth produced a weird sound, a kind of snarl, full of pain and jealousy. Aunt Martha turned her back on the room disdainfully. *Jealousy?*

'Is he gone mad or what?' Granny Godkin demanded, glaring petulantly at the two women. She liked to start these fights and then pretend that those who fought with her were unreasonable to the point of insanity. 'The DTs,' she muttered. 'Definitely.'

'O shut up!' Aunt Martha cried, and plunged her hands into her hair. Michael, not without amusement, craned his neck and peered down at the wine stains on his back. Papa returned. He had straightened his tie and brushed his hair and sponged the mud from his suit. He took his place at the head of the table. Aunt Martha remained standing for a time, uncertain whether or not the row was finished, glaring histrionically at my father. He ignored her, and she sat down. Josie brought in the coffee.

'Well, men,' said Papa, glancing at Michael and me. 'Blackers tomorrow, eh? All set?'

57

'Yes, Uncle Joe.'

'That's good, that's good.' He nodded vigorously, spooning sugar into his cup. 'It's a fair crop this year.'

What surprises me even still is that his heartiness was only slightly false, and only that much because he did not know how to talk to youngsters. The shouting and the broken bottle, all that was as nothing. Mama started the milkjug on its journey around the table. Granny Godkin was made to take her pill. Aunt Martha yawned behind her fingers.

'A fair crop,' Papa said again, and buried his nose in his cup. Michael glanced at me. I heard Josie rattling pots in the kitchen. Darkness pressed softly against the windows. The night was still and calm in its reaches, with a promise of fair weather for the morrow. Humankind is extraordinary.

PAPA WAS RIGHT, the blackcurrant crop was the heaviest in years that year. Just as well, since the fruit was by now one of the last remaining sources of income at Birchwood. The land on which it flourished had been already sold, and this was the final harvest we would take. Michael and I were put in charge of the pickers, a ragged army of tenant children and their grandmothers, and a few decrepit old men no longer capable of heavier toil. They were a wild primitive bunch, the old people half crazed by the weight of their years, the children as cheerfully vicious as young animals. Their conversation dwelt almost to the exclusion of all else on sex and death, and the children managed a neat conjunction of the two by carrying on their lovelife after dark in the local graveyard. They shied away instinctively from me, found me cold, I suppose, or saw my father in me, but Michael they immediately accepted. That surprised me. They listened to his orders and, more startling still, did as he told them. They even offered to arrange a girlfriend for him. That offer he declined, for he had little interest in the sexual duet, being a confirmed soloist, and it was I who made a conquest, when I met Rosie.

In the morning I rose early and waded down through pools of sleep on the stairs to the garden, where Michael waited for me in the cart with Nockter. The lawn was drenched with light, the trees in the wood were still. A bright butterfly darned the air above the horse's head. We rattled along violet-shadowed lanes quick with blackbirds, by the edges of meadows where the corn was bursting. Birdsong shook the wood like gushes of wind. All was still but for the small clouds sailing their courses, and it was

59

pleasant to be abroad in that new morning, with the smell of the furze, and the grass sparkling, that hawk, all these things.

We reached the plantation. Nockter set up the huge brass scales, and Michael unharnessed the horse, whispering in its ear. I heard beyond the clatter of metal and leather the distant ring of voices, and turned and saw, down the long meadow, a concourse approaching, trembling on the mist, their cries softly falling through the air, mysterious and gay. If only, when they were beside me, when I was among them, they had retained even a fragment of the beauty of that first vision, I might have loved them. It is ever thus.

The fruit we hardly picked, but rather saved. From under their canopies of leaf the heavy purple clusters tumbled with a kind of abandon into our hands. Down in the green gloom under the bushes, where spiders swarmed, the berries were gorgeous, achingly vivid against the dusty leaves, but once plucked, and in the baskets, their burnished lustre faded and a moist whitish film settled on the skin. If they were to be eaten, and we ate them by the handful at the start, it was only in that shocked moment of separation from the stems that they held their true, their unearthly flavour. Then the fat beads burst on our tongues with a chill bitterness which left our eyelids damp and our mouths flooded, a bitterness which can still pierce my heart, for it is the very taste of time.

Rosie was there with her granny, an obese old woman whose coarse tongue and raucous cackle froze the child into a trance of embarrassment. I noticed her first when we paused at noon to eat our sandwiches. Michael and I lay in the long grass of a ditch, belching and sighing, contemplating our outstretched bare legs and grimy toes. Rosie sat a little way from us, daintily fighting three persistent flies for possession of a cream bun. She had short dark hair rolled into hideous sausage curls. A saddle of freckles sat on her nose. She wore sandals and a dress with daisies on it. She was pretty, a sturdy sunburned creature. Having won her bun, she wiped the corners of her mouth with her fingertips and began to eat blackcurrants from the basket beside her, slowly, one by one, drawing back her lips and bursting each berry between her tiny white teeth. A trickle of crimson juice ran down her chin and dropped, plop, into her lap, staining a yellow daisy pink.

We went back to work then. I heard her granny's laughter

rising over the meadow, and by some mysterious process that awful noise was transmuted into an audible expression of the excitement which was making my hands tremble and my heart race.

So at every noon we drew a little nearer to each other, treading our way like swimmers toward that bright island which we did not reach until the last day of the harvest, when the weights were totted and the wages paid, and under cover of the general gaiety she sidled up to me, stood for a long time in a tense silence, and then abruptly said,

'I made sevenanatanner.'

She opened her fist and showed me the moist coins lying on her palm. I pursed my lips and gravely nodded, and gazed away across the fields, trying to look as though I were struggling with some great and terrible thought. At our feet Michael sat with his back against the wheel of the cart, slowly munching an enormous sandwich. He glanced up at us briefly, with a faint trace of mockery. Rosie stirred and sighed, trapped her hands behind her back, and began to grind the toe of her sandal into the grass. Her knees were stippled with rich red scratches, crescents of blood-beads.

'That's fourteen stone,' she said, and added faintly, 'and two pound.'

That was more than I had picked, and I was about to admit as much when abruptly Michael bounced up between us, coughed, hitched up his trousers, and grinned at the horse. The shock of this apparition made our eyes snap back into focus, and the others around us materialised again, and the wave of jabbering voices and the jingle of money swelled in our ears. Rosie blushed and sadly, slowly, paced stiff-legged away.

I helped Nockter to dismantle the scales, and we loaded the pieces on the cart while Michael harnessed the horse. The pickers drifted off into the lowering sun. We followed them across the meadow and then turned away toward home. Nockter clicked his tongue at the horse and rattled the reins along its back. Michael and I walked in silence beside the rolling cart. He was wearing Nockter's hat pushed down on the back of his head. We reached the lane. I was thinking that if Michael had not popped up between us like that, the clown, I might have, I could have, why, I *would* have—Rosie stepped out of a bush at the side of the lane ahead of us, tugging at her dress. My heart! She gaped at us, greatly flustered, started off in one direction, turned, tried the other, stopped. The cart rumbled on. Nockter grinned. Michael began to whistle. I hesitated, doing a kind of agonised dance in my embarrassment, and finally stood still. She smiled timidly. A massed choir of not altogether sober cherubim burst into song. I felt ridiculous.

'You're gas,' said Rosie.

She came to me at Cotter's place that evening with a shower of rain behind her. The drops fell like fire through the dying copper light of day. All of the wood was aflame. She had wanted me to meet her in the graveyard, like any normal swain. I drew the line there.

WHEN I WAS with Rosie it seemed enough simply to be there—if one can ever be anywhere simply—but time complicates everything. Over the years the memory of our affair, that aching fugue of swoons and smiles, has dwindled to a motionless golden point whose texture in the surrounding gloom is that of sunblurred skin redolent of crushed grass and flowers, which Alessandro di Mariano knew so well, the texture of seraphs' wings. Beside all this, the actuality of my peasant girlchild with her grubby nails and sausage curls seems a tawdry thing, and I suppose it is not her but an iridescent ideal that I remember. Try as I will, I cannot see her face. Her other parts, or some of them, I vividly recall, naturally. That evening, or another, in the wood, we talked for a while with excessive gravity and great difficulty and then, glumly, surrendered to the silence. Things were looking very bad when I played what turned out to my surprise to be a trump. I told her about algebra. She stared at me with open mouth and huge eyes as I revealed to her the secrets of this amazing new world, mine, where figures, your old pals, *figgers*, yes, were put through outlandish and baffling exercises. Let x equal *whaa*...? Ah yes, I won her heart with mathematics. She was still pondering those mysterious symbols, her lips moving incredulously, when I delved between her chill pale thighs and discovered there her own, frail secret. She snapped her legs shut like a trap and scuttled out of my clutches, sat back on her heels and gazed at me with moony eyes, distraught, reproachful, shocked, aye, and tumescent.

'*You dirty thing,*' she whispered.

Our affair, then, was founded on mutual astonishment at the intricacy of things, my brain, her cunt, things like that. Affair, that word again. I must not exaggerate. We parted virgins. Still I do not deny, I do not deny what she meant to me. I wandered about the house and garden in a mad mist, blind to everything but the hands of the clock which, with their agonisingly slow semaphore, dragged the evening toward me across the ticking dry bones of the day. Birchwood and its inmates were disintegrating around me, and I hardly noticed.

Papa's jaunts to the city had become rare, and lately had ceased altogether. He displayed a new and, to me, disturbing interest in the house, almost an obsession. One day he announced a plan to have the place repaired. He would pay the builder with an acre of timber. *Capital notion!* He went into town to see about it, and came home drunk, in great good humour, the renovations forgotten. That very night the schoolroom ceiling collapsed, and when Michael and I went to investigate with Mama, the swaying light of our candles showed us, up in the rotten cavity, a decayed hanging forest of rank green growths stirring like seaweed in the swell of crossdraughts. We locked away that horrible aquarium, and in the morning Papa's headache would allow no mention of catastrophe. Two boards in the lavatory floor crumbled to dust under him on a silent Sunday morning, leaving him perched on the bowl, instantly constipated, his feet and crumpled trousers dangling above an abyss.

'Nockter! Jesus Christ almighty. *Nock*—there you are. Get me a hammer, nails, a couple of planks, hurry up, we have a job to do. I could have been killed. Like that! Jesus can you imagine the laugh they'd have. *Broke his arse on his own lav, ha!*' He glared at us darkly, daring us to laugh, but in spite of all his fierceness I noticed again now what I had noticed for the first time recently, that he had begun to shrink, I do not mean in my estimation, but in his own stature, as if something inside him, some of his stuffings, had fallen out, and I could not help thinking of a sucked brittle carcase of a wasp, neatly parcelled in paste, enmeshed in a spider's web. 'This will have to stop, have to,' he cried. 'The bloody house is coming down around our ears.' But before the tools were brought he had taken his gun and stalked off into the wood, running his hands through his hair and muttering under his breath, and I had slipped away to meet my love.

A soft hot haze, lilac, burnt gold, yellow, lay under the trees in the wood. The birds sang, dragonflies hovered above the briars. The butterflies were all gone. Summer was ending. Rosie waited for me in the shadow under Cotter's wall, sitting with her head dreamily drooping, her lithe brown legs folded under her, as I sometimes see her still in dreams, leaning on one taut curved arm, twisting and twisting a stalk of grass around her fingers. She gave me from under her long lashes that glance of inexplicable resentment which never failed to reduce me to a trembling ingratiating jelly. Inexplicable? No. One needed only to hear our accents to begin to understand. Class sat silent and immovable between us like a large black bird.

We walked through the goldengreen wood. The leaves were turning already. At a sudden bend in a long-untrodden path we came abruptly, magically, to the edge of the lake, and stopped and gazed out across a prospect of summer and peace, the ashblue water, the house, the windows brimming with light, and two little figures walking slowly up the steps to the front door. Birchwood always took itself too seriously, turning its face away from the endless intricate farce being enacted under its roof, but on its good days, when one was willing to accept it on its own terms, it was magnificent. Rosie twisted her mouth thoughtfully, squinting at all that quiet grandeur, and produced with a wry flourish a comment that seemed somehow the most fitting one imaginable.

'If my granny seen me now, she'd kill me.'

Yes indeed, and if mine saw me. We wandered along the lake shore to the summerhouse, soberly musing on the punishments our furtive venery could call down upon us. She sat down in the ancient rocking-chair on the porch and stared past me with narrowed eyes.

'All them *swanks*,' she said suddenly, and sniffed, all that envy, that violent longing. I frowned, pretending that I had not understood her, but I knew well what she was after. Here was a perilous situation. The country was up in arms. Every day there were reports of our people burned out of their farms, of constabulary men beaten up, of magistrates shot in the streets. It all seemed far away at first, then an old man spat on Aunt Martha in the town, and Josie, to her great amusement, answered a dreadful banging on the front door one early morning and found one of our own chickens nailed to it, and now here was I, faced with a miniature rebellion of my own. I understood her well enough. Did she seriously think that I would let her meet my family, those mysterious and splendid swanks? Good god. There flashed before me a picture of the two of us advancing down the drawing room toward Granny Godkin on her throne by the fire, a Granny Godkin whom the prospects of fury and derision she perceived in the uprising had rejuvenated, whose shrill broken voice had begun to ring again through the house with something like its old authority, and as that horrible thought was exploding within me slowly I slowly clambered up the railing, grasped the clogged drainpipe above and hung before her, swaying slightly, a solemn baboon. She regarded me with a sullen eye, then flung herself from the chair and kicked open the door of the summerhouse. I flopped to the floor and followed her.

This place, cluttered more than ever with migratory bits and sticks from across the lake, we had not dared to enter before. It was a perilous forbidden chapel in our wood locked to us by the spell of Granny Godkin and her wicked cards. Our visit, therefore, was something of an occasion, and prompted in me frightful thoughts. We climbed the curving stairs at the back to a little room above, where there was a broken bed, two crippled chairs, and a curlicued gilt mirror, filthy but intact, a patient spy which now inclined its purblind eye upon my country darling, who poked among the junk with wrinkled nose. I hovered behind her like a nervous vampire and kissed her hot neck. She hardly noticed me, but twisted absently out of my reach and with graceful flamingo steps danced to the window, singing.

Chase me Charlie
I've got barley
Up the leg of me
drawers.

But there, by the glass, in the misty light, her mood shifted and she turned, suddenly transformed, and her scattered drugged smile touched me here and there like a small furry blind animal. She took a slow step, another, swimming through air, and without a word put her arms around me, and I seem to have fallen over backwards slowly, lost in that world contained in the tender roseate canthus of her eye. Perhaps it was love, after all. Beyond and above her blurred left temple a tiny redhaired phantom rippled into the depths of the mirror. She sensed my fright, and looked wildly over her shoulder at the glass. We crawled on hands and knees to the window, laid our noses on the sill and cautiously peered out. Down by the lake's edge Michael stood, looking toward the trees. Did I glimpse there a figure retreating into the leaves, an arm lifted in a hieratic gesture of farewell? I went down the stairs. Michael, coming in at the door, halted with the light behind him.

'O, it's you,' he said coolly. 'Gave me a fright.' Rosie went down past me, her head bowed, hands behind her, busy with her curls. As she passed him by, Michael glanced at her and then at me and permitted himself a brief grin. We went, all three, out into the glowing noon.

'Well, I'm off,' Rosie muttered, without looking back.

Michael and I stared at each other, teetering, as it were, on the edge of a revelation, and, who knows, we might have bared our hearts had there not come at that moment, beside us, or so it seemed, the shattering blast of a shotgun followed by a scream. Rosie was crouched by the edge of the trees with her head in her hands, and off to her left there was Papa, legs braced wide apart, smoking gun to his shoulder, a ridiculously stylised illustration of the archetypal hunter. Rosie sank to her knees, cowering in fright, with her arms still around her head. She lifted one elbow and peered out at him from under it. He looked from her to us, to the girl again. His moustache twitched, and one eyebrow jumped up his forehead. He lowered the gun, stood undecided for a moment, and then backed off into the trees, bowing under the boughs. Rosie began to howl. Michael softly laughed.

SUMMER ENDED OFFICIALLY with the lighting of a fire in the drawing room. Rain fell all day, big sad drops drumming on the dead leaves, and smoke billowed back down the chimneys, where rooks had nested. The house seemed huge, hollow, all emptiness and echo. In the morning Granny Godkin was discovered in the hall struggling with an umbrella which would not open. She was going down to the summerhouse, rain or no rain, and when they tried to restrain her she shook her head and muttered, and rattled the umbrella furiously. In the last weeks, after her brief vibrant interval of fanged gaiety when the prospect appeared of a peasant revolt, she had become strangely withdrawn and vague, wandering distractedly about the house, sighing and sometimes even quietly weeping. She said there was no welcome for her now at Birchwood —a remark I wish to stress, for reasons which I will presently disclose—and spent more and more time down at the lake despite the autumnal damp. Often Michael and I would see her sitting motionless by the table in the summerhouse, her head inclined and her eyes intently narrowed, listening to the subtle shifts and subsidences within her, the mechanism of her body winding down.

'But you'll catch your death,' Mama cried. 'It's teeming.'

'What?' the old woman snapped. 'What? Leave me alone.'

'But—'

'Let me *be*, will you.'

Mama turned to my father. 'Joe, can you not...? She'll get her death...' As always when she spoke to him now her voice dwindled hopelessly, sadly, and in silence her eyes, moist with tenderness and despair, followed him as he shrugged indifferently

68

and turned away wearily to shut himself into the drawing room.

'*Curse you, will you open,*' Granny Godkin snarled, and thwacked the brolly like a whip. Mama, with her pathetic faith in reason, opened wide the front door to show the old woman the wickedness of the weather. 'Look, look how bad it is. You'll be drenched.'

Granny Godkin paused, and grinned slyly, wickedly, and glanced up sideways at Mama.

'You worry?' she whispered. 'Heh!'

The grin became a skeletal sneer, and she glared about her at the hall, and suddenly the umbrella flew open, a strange glossy black blossom humming on its struts, and when I think of that day it is that black flower dipping and bobbing in the gloomy hall which recalls the horror best. The old woman thrust it before her out the door, where a sudden gust of wind snatched it up and she was swept down the steps, across the lawn, and I ducked into the library to avoid Mama's inevitable, woebegone embrace.

Aunt Martha waited for me, huddled in an armchair by the empty fireplace with a shawl around her shoulders, gazing blankly at a book open in her lap and gnawing a raw carrot. She hardly looked at me, but flung the carrot into the grate and began to whine at once.

'Where have you been? I'm waiting this hour. Do you think I've nothing better to do? Your father says you're to learn Latin, I don't know why, god only knows, but there you are. Look at this book. Amo amas amat, love. Say it, amo, come on. Amo, I love.'

I sat and looked at her with that serene silent stare which never failed to drive her into a frenzy. She slapped the primer shut and bared her teeth, an unpleasant habit she had when angry, just like Papa.

'You know you really are a horrible little boy, do you know that, do you? Why do you hate me? I spend half my life in this house trying to give you some kind of an education, and all you do is gawp and grin—O yes, I've seen you grinning, you you you...' She clapped a hand to her forehead and closed her eyes. 'O, I, I must... Look, come, try to learn something, look at this lovely language, these words, Gabriel, please, for me, for your Mama, you're a dear child. Now, amo, I love...'

But she shut the book again, and with a low moan looked

fretfully around the room, searching for something to which she might anchor her fractured attention. It occurred to me that my presence made hardly any difference to her, I mean she would have carried on like this whether I was there or not, might even have talked all that nonsense to the empty air. They were all fleeing into themselves, as fast as they could flee, all my loved ones. At the dinner table now I could gaze at any or all of them without ever receiving in return an inquiring glance, or an order to eat up and stop staring, or even a sad smile from Mama. Even Michael had since that day at the summerhouse become silent and preoccupied, had begun to avoid me, and I felt sure that he knew some secret which involved me and which I was not to know. I was like a lone survivor wandering among the wreckage, like Tiresias in the city of plague.

Papa insinuated himself into the room, slipped in at the door and tiptoed to the window without looking at us, and there stood gazing out at the dripping trees, rocking slowly on his heels, a gloomy ghost. Aunt Martha appeared not to have noticed him. She tapped my knee peremptorily with her fist.

'You must learn, Gabriel, it's no good to—'

The room shook. There was no sound, but instead a sensation of some huge thing crumpling, like a gargantuan heart attack, that part of an explosion that races out in a wave ahead of the blast and buckles the silence. But the blast did not arrive, and Aunt Martha looked at the ceiling, and Papa glanced at us querulously over his shoulder, and we said nothing. Perhaps we had imagined it, like those peals of thunder that wrench us out of sleep on calm summer nights. The world is full of inexplicable noises, yelps and howls, the echoes of untold disasters.

'It's no good to just sit and say nothing, Gabriel,' said Aunt Martha. 'You must learn things, we all had to learn, and it's not so difficult. Mensa is a table, see? Mensa...'

While she talked, Papa made his way across the room by slow degrees, casually, his lips pursed, until he stood behind her chair looking down over her shoulder at the book and jingling coins in his pocket. She fell silent, and sat very still with her head bent over the page, and Papa hummed a tune and walked out of the room, and she put down the primer and followed him, and I was left alone, wondering where and when all this had happened before.

I picked up the book she had dropped and humbed glumly through it. The words lay dead in ranks, file beside file of slaughtered music. I rescued one, that verb to love, and, singing its parts in a whisper, I lifted my eyes to the window. Nockter, his elbows sawing, knees pumping, came running across the lawn. It was so perfect a picture of bad news arriving, this little figure behind the rainstippled glass looming out of wind and violence, that at first I took it to be no more than a stray fancy born of boredom. I looked again. He slipped on the grass, frantically backpedalling an imaginary bicycle, and plunged abruptly arse over tip out of my view amid a sense of general hilarity. I waited, and sure enough a few moments later the house quivered with the first groundswell of catastrophe. Nockter appeared in my window again, limping back the way he had come, with my father now by his side, his coattails flying. Next came poor Mama, struggling against the wind and, last of all, in a pink dressing gown, Aunt Martha. They dived into the wood, one after another, but when they were gone the shaking and shuddering of the stormtossed garden seemed an echo of their tempestuous panic. Michael entered quietly behind me.

'What's up?' he asked.

I did not know, and hardly cared. It was not for me to question this splendid spectacle of consternation in the adult camp. I was not a cruel child, only a cold one, and I feared boredom above all else. So we clasped our hands behind our backs and gazed out into the rain, awaiting the next act. Soon they came back, straggling despondently in reverse order, Aunt Martha, Mama, and then Nockter and my father. They passed by the window with downcast eyes.

'We should...' Michael began. He eyed me speculatively, biting bits off a thumbnail. 'Do you think she's...?'

The hall. I remember it so well, that scene, so vividly. My father was stooped over the phone, rattling the cradle with a frenzied forefinger and furiously shaking the earpiece, but the thing would not speak to him. His hair was in his eyes, his knees trembled. Mama, with one hand on her forehead and the other stretched out to the table behind her for support, leaned backwards in a half swoon, her lips parted and eyelids drooping, her drenched hair hanging down her back. Nockter sat, caked with mud from his fall, on the edge of a little chair, looking absurdly stolid and calm, almost detached. The front door stood open. Three dead leaves were busy chasing each other round and round on the carpet. I saw all this in a flash, and no doubt that precise situation took no more than an instant to swell and flow into another, but for me it is petrified forever, the tapping finger, Mama's dripping hair, those leaves. Aunt Martha, in her ruined pink frilly, was slowly ascending the stairs backwards. The fall of her foot on each new step shook her entire frame as the tendons tugged on a web of connections, and her jaws slackened, her chest heaved, while out of her mouth there fell curious little high-pitched grunts, which were so abrupt, so understated, that I imagined them as soft furry balls of sound falling to the carpet and lodging in the nap. Up she went, and up, until there were no more steps, and she sat down on the highest one with a bump and buried her face in her hands, and at last an ethereal voice in the phone answered Papa's pleas with a shrill hoot.

My memory is curious, a magpie with a perverse eyes, it fascinates me. Jewels I remember only as glitter, and the feel of glass in my beak. I have filled my nest with dross. What does it mean? That is a question I am forever asking, what can it mean? There is never a precise answer, but instead, in the sky, as it were, a kind of jovian nod, a celestial tipping of the wink, *that's all right, it means what it means.* Yes, but is that enough? Am I satisfied? I wonder. That day I remember Nockter falling, Mama running across the garden in the rain, that scene in the hall, all those things, whereas, listen, what I should recall to the exclusion of all else is the scene in the summerhouse that met Michael and me when we sneaked down there, the ashes on the wall, that rendered purplish mass in the chair, Granny Godkin's two feet, all that was left of her, in their scorched button boots, and I do remember it, in a sense, as words, as facts, but I cannot see it, and there is the trouble. Well, perhaps it is better thus. I have no wish to make unseemly disclosures about myself, and I can never think of that ghastly day without suspecting that somewhere inside me some cruel little brute, a manikin in my mirror, is bent double with laughter. Granny! Forgive me.

WE MISSED HER, in a way. When Granda Godkin died it was like the shamefaced departure of a ghost who no longer frightens. That tiresome clank of bones was no more to be heard in the hall, the wicked laughter on the landing was silenced. The space he had occupied closed in, making a little more room for the rest of us, and we stretched ourselves and heaved a small sigh, and were secretly relieved. But when the old woman was so unceremoniously snuffed out something fretful entered the house. Now there was always something wrong with the stillness. Our chairs seemed to vibrate, a ceaseless tremor under our backsides would not let us sit, and we went wandering from room to room like old dogs sniffing moodily after their dead master. The house seemed incomplete, as often a room did when Mama, on one of her restless days, shifted out of it a piece of furniture which had stood in the same place for so long that it was only noticed in its absence. Birchwood was diminished, there is no denying it.

The arranging of her funeral gave rise to some moments of bleak comedy. That was really awful, for we could not in decency laugh. How was she to be buried, anyway? Were we to call in the undertakers to scrape what little was left of her out of the chair, off the walls? No no, if the ghastly manner of her death got out the town would burst with merriment. Well then, were we to do it ourselves? God forbid! An unspeakable vision arose of the family donning dungarees and gumboots and trooping off to the summerhouse with buckets and trowels. Never had the euphemism *the remains* seemed more apt.

The situation itself was bad enough, but it was made doubly

difficult by the virtual impossibility of talking about it. Apart from the unmentionable horror of the old woman's death, each of us was tonguetied by the fact that we were convinced that the others knew exactly how she had died, that it was ridiculously obvious, that our own bafflement was laughable. We became very cunning in our efforts to quiz each other. The fishing! How we sighed, and played with our fingers, and glared solemnly out of windows during those awful plummeting silences between casts. *The poor thing, it must have been terrible—to go like that!* Yes, terrible. *Do you think...?* No no, no, I wouldn't... *Still, she must have known...* O there's no doubt— *But still—* Yes? Yes? *Exactly!* And at the end, no wiser, we parted morosely, guiltily, furious with ourselves.

Doc McCabe was the only one to offer an explanation, and although it was too scandalous and too simple in its way for my family to accept, I think he may have been right. He arrived in the afternoon, huffing and puffing, trailing rainwater behind him from the ends of his cape, an overweight tweedy ball of irritation. He had attended two hysterical and protracted births that day, and now he pronounced himself banjaxed. Before anyone could speak he lumbered over to my chair, wrenched my jaws open and glared down my throat.

'Touch of the grippe. Be over it in a day or two. Well?'

The constraint in the atmosphere at last made an impression on him, and he looked around at the rest of them with his eyebrows quivering. Apparently he had not heard of Granny Godkin's departure. We marched down to the summerhouse, the tribe leading their medicine man to the evil spirit. The rain stopped and the sun appeared abruptly. We waited outside on the porch in an embarrassed silence while he went in to investigate. After what seemed an age the door opened and he backed out slowly, his head bent, fingers to his lips. He was intrigued.

'*Extraordinary*. Upon my word, I've never come across anything like it...' He found the bereaved family watching him with a suitably muted air of expectation, and he coughed and turned away abruptly, humming and hawing under his breath. We trooped back to the house, and there, in the dining room, swilling tea, his curiosity got the better of him again, and he had trouble preventing himself from grinning enthusiastically as he mused upon that strange death.

'Most extraordinary, really. I've read of one or two similar cases, you know, in America, if I remember rightly, but I never thought'—he scoffed at his lack of foresight—'dear me, I never thought that here...that Birchwood...' He looked about with a newfound air of respect at this humble and familiar place that had produced such a marvel. 'Not a mark anywhere, only the chair. Can't have been a fire, discount that absolutely. Those smuts on the wall...' Aunt Martha let fall a muffled sob, and the old boy glanced at her apologetically. 'But it's terrible, of course, very sad, it must have been a great shock, indeed yes, ahem.'

He put down his cup, and with a promise to *tip the wink* to the coroner he prepared to depart. Papa tackled him in the hall.

'Well you think then, Doctor...? I mean...?'

'Eh?' He cast a wary eye over Papa's shoulder at Aunt Martha's puffed tear-stained face. 'Well of course until I examine it further... I may have to call in some people from Dublin. At the moment, however, I can see no other explanation...after all...'

'Yes?'

The old shammer sniffed, and fussed with the collar of his cape. He turned to the door, paused, and cast one bloodshot eye back over his shoulder at us.

'*Spontaneous combustion*,' he said faintly, dived out on the step, and with a last embarrassed grunt was gone. As I say, he may have been right, she may have just...burst, but I cannot rid myself of the notion that the house itself had something to do with it. Birchwood had grown weary of her, she saw that herself. Did it assassinate her? Extraordinary, as the Doc observed.

He did speak to the coroner, and a vague verdict of death by misadventure was returned, but for this service he expected to be allowed to conduct the people he had called in from Dublin, old cronies of his, around the scene of the disaster, and was greatly incensed when Papa refused entry to him and his band of ghouls. However, he kept our secret from the town. In a week or two there was hardly anything of the incident left, except Josie's mournful sobbing at odd hours of the day and night, for she came up trumps and surprised us all by displaying genuine grief for the old woman's passing. By the way, we settled the business of the funeral very neatly, and buried Granny Godkin's feet in a full-sized coffin. Despite the needless expense, the craftiness of the ruse pleased Papa enormously.

OLD MCCABE MAY have been right about Granny Godkin, but he was quite wrong about my touch of grippe. In fact, it blossomed into an impressive dose of pneumonia. All day I had felt curiously isolated, as though I were enclosed in a very fine transparent membrane. Loud noises came to me muffled, whereas the tiniest sound, a match striking, say, was like a thunderclap. I pretended to be quite well, in spite of the Doc's diagnosis, which had galvanised Mama into a paroxysm of concern, and it was with great difficulty that I avoided having that evil-tasting thermometer thrust into the throbbing velvet under my tongue. I feared being put to bed, for the ramifications of the old woman's fiery finish were too good to miss, and anyway I had a date with Rosie.

Now that the summer was ended our affair had run into difficulties. We had no shelter. The empty stables behind the kitchen were dangerously close to the house, and Nockter nearly caught us on our one bold visit to the hayshed. We went back to Cotter's place and prayed for some disaster on the sun to turn our autumn into a searing indian summer. Our prayers, as we had gloomily expected, went unanswered. These material difficulties, however, were only the tip of the iceberg that had begun to rise between us. Our idyll was ending. The strange fact is that we were not drawing apart, on the contrary, we were beginning to get to know one another. We had each dreamed a lover for ourselves, but dreams are brittle things, and piggish reality tramples them to bits under its trotters. Now, as we peered through the thinning mist, we perceived in each other disconcerting little habits which, it is true, we had already noticed, but they had been sublimely un-important. She picked her nose with a kind of venom when think-ing deeply, and sometimes her laughter struck an unsettling echo of her grandmother's raucous cackle. Things like that. I clearly remember the unwarranted intensity of my shock when I dis-covered under her left armpit a sinister chocolate-brown mole. And I imagine that the variety of ways in which I disillusioned her must have been impressive. We saw us as we were, and the sight was hardly to be borne.

Late that evening the wind abated, but the rain began to fall again in half-hearted flurries, and the trees now and then dropped a clatter of tears. Rosie, wrapped in a gleaming black raincoat, wore her brother's wellingtons and a yellow hat, and all I could touch were her chill damp face and etiolated hands. I huddled against her under Cotter's wall, shaking like a drunk. Those moments were perversely sweet. My hair stood on end each time she dipped her tongue into my throbbing mouth. At last, infuriated by my groans, she pushed me away. Nothing rages like a fourteen-year-old scorned.

'*What are you crying for?*'

It was rain on my face, not tears. I grinned, to show her how well I was.

'You're just playacting. You don't like me any more. Well I don't like you much any more either! Just because I'm not *grand* enough for you.'

That was how it was now. She ran away through the trees, holding her hat in place with one hand and stumbling in her outsize boots. I made no effort to stop her. I had arrived at that stage of illness where my weariness was such that it seemed I had all day been playing all the parts in a nonstop show, Rosie was right there, did she but know it, I had been Granny Godkin exploding, Nockter falling, the telephonist hooting, Rosie fleeing, Gabriel struggling with his ague, and now I was tired of it all, they would have to play their own parts without me, for I was retiring from the boards. Fever was the only reality. I rattled miserably home, and there, like the pale boy in a cautionary illustration, I fell into Mama's arms, a drenched waif.

That night was horrible. I wallowed in a hot noisome sweat that smelled of rotten roses, grinding my teeth and shivering. A small toadlike animal seemed to have lodged itself in my trachea, and at every cough it plunged a quivering claw into my left lung. The room seemed thronged until the early hours with unbearably busy nurses. Mama would lean over me in the bilious yellow lamplight, trumpeting incoherently, and then another, Aunt Martha perhaps, would fling open the door, sweep up to the bed and thrust her rubbery face down on mine. There was a troubling dichotomy between their frenetic activity and their voices, for all sound had slowed down to an underwater pace, an intermittent booming in my ears broken into regular beats whose rhythm, I suspect, corresponded to the fretful flutter of my pulse. I swung vertiginously in and out of sleep, and at last subsided into something which was not sleep, but rather a comatose sentry duty over my quietly pulsating body.

I swam up slowly out of that murky sea into a calm bright morning. The light in the room was of the palest blue and gold, extraordinarily steady. It seemed to come from everywhere at once, as though each surface were the source of its own illumination. On the table by my bed a single red rose, mysterious and perfect, stood in a glass. The stem seemed fractured where it entered the bluish water. A deep stillness reigned, originating in the centre of my forehead and radiating out through room after room, holding the life of the house in thrall. I lay on my back in this floating florentine world and gazed into the white infinity of the ceiling. I felt as fragile as fine glass, neutral, numb except for my hair, which crackled painfully when I turned my head on the pillow, and even that minute torment was no more than the stab of anguish which pierces the heart when one is faced with something of incomparable beauty, as I was then, a beauty which did not spring from any one thing, but from every thing, causing the light to sing. I have experienced that same sensation only once or twice since then, in these nights, in my latest sickness, toiling over these words.

And as in this present toil too was the way that day in which my fevered brain was working. I went back through many years, as many as I could remember, gathering fragments of evidence, feeling my way around certain discrepancies, retrieving chance words let drop and immediately picked up again, collating all those scraps that pointed unmistakeably, as I now saw, to one awesome and abiding fact, namely, that somewhere I had a sister, my twin, a lost child. This discovery filled me with excitement, but I could not say whether the excitement was produced by the cool and lucid manner in which I marshalled the evidence or by the conclusion which I had reached, and that troubled me. But a sister! Half of me, somewhere, stolen by the circus, or spirited away by an evil aunt, or kidnapped by a jealous cousin—and why? A part of me stolen, yes, that was a thrilling notion. I was incomplete, and would remain so until I found her. All this was real to me, and perfectly reasonable.

Someone in the corridor tried the handle of the door. The sound floated through the hollow silence like the chiming of polished steel pipes. Footsteps boomed away into an enormous distance, fell silent, and then returned. This time the door opened, and another door, in the mirror of my wardrobe, flew open on another world out of which Aunt Martha stepped and laid her cold hand on my forehead.

'O you're on fire, on fire!'

A petal fell from the rose beside me.

I recovered in a week or two. They told me that I had been delirious. I had no reason to disbelieve them, except that I had not invented Granny Godkin's death, or any of the events of that first day of fever, and I knew that if I had not invented all that, had not played out all those parts in my burning brain, then anything was possible.

IT WAS A hard winter, no harder than in other years, I suppose, but the house was dying, and the cold got in, the fierce winds and fiercer frost. Flocks of slates flew off the roof, rain seeped into the bedrooms. One morning my water sizzled on a film of ice in the second floor lavatory, the only one that worked now. From that time there comes back to me above all the taste of porridge and the feel of damp blankets.

Papa no longer tried to hide his helplessness. He gazed on the dissolution of his kingdom in a kind of daze, humming distractedly under his breath. He was rarely sober, and sometimes at night I would hear him stumbling up the stairs, cursing and belching, and kicking over the jamjars which Mama had so carefully placed under the leaks in the ceilings. Nockter disappeared one night, and in the morning the police came looking for him. It seems he was in the movement. Papa was profoundly shocked. The rot of rebellion was no longer distant and therefore manageable, but had spread under his own roof, had flourished among the innocent flowers of Birchwood. I remember him, in his armchair in the library, gingerly opening the morning newspaper, holding his face away from it as though he feared that a fist might lash out from between the pages and punch him on the nose, and then there was his look of awe and bafflement as he read of the latest disasters and assassinations. Surely it was all a dream? The world was solid, god damn it! He began to watch Josie with a brooding eye, and engaged her in elaborate and roundabout conversations meant to test her loyalty, but which only amused her, and left her convinced that he was losing his reason. Then he made the most frightful discovery of all, that old man Lawless, Mama's father, was now in possession of a large share of Birchwood. Every acre that Papa had sold he had sold unwittingly to his father-in-law, who, as usual, had worked in silence and stealth, using the Gadderns and the other buyers, all cronies, as his unofficial agents. Mama was mortified, and protested her innocence, but Papa, without a word, only a look, accused her of complicity. He saw betrayals everywhere. Poor Papa.

Now that Nockter was gone, Rosie and I went back to the hayshed, and in that furry warm haven our passion blazed again briefly. Once or twice I tried to talk to Michael about her. He was not interested. In the last months he had changed, had become even more reticent, which meant that he hardly spoke at all. The mockery in his smile was now directed openly at all of us, but it was always mockery, never contempt, and there was something else, buried deep within him, wistfulness, longing, I don't know. He remains for me still, yes, even still, a secretive and troubled creature with a knot of thorns in his heart. Or is that only how I wish to remember him?

Mama instituted economy drives. They got nowhere, and probably put a greater strain on the budget than our usual profligacy. Her oddest venture was to dig out from god knows what musty corners our castoff clothes so that we might get one last wear out of them before they fell to pieces. We disappointed her by stoutly refusing, amid not wholly convincing guffaws, to deck ourselves out in these eerie echoes from the past, and it was left to her to trail through the house a bizarre parody of the weekend parties and hunt balls of immemorial seasons. The clothes had a chilling but, now that I think of it, not unexpected effect upon her. She began, in subtle ways, to play the part that the costume of the day demanded, and how uneasy was the silence that settled on the dining room when she swept to the table in a purple velvet evening gown, or came tripping down in a gossamer frock straight out of the gay nineties.

Snow fell on Christmas Day, as it is supposed to do. All morning, out of a low sky, the big white flakes flowed down, silent, mysterious, muffling everything. The house ached with boredom. For my Christmas box Aunt Martha gave me a stamp album, and I spent a pleasantly demented hour in my room ripping it slowly, lovingly, to shreds. At noon the snow made a determined effort to stop, and Josie served ham sandwiches and stewed tea and tacky mince pies. Michael trudged off toward the town. I tormented the grandfather clock in the hall, turning the hands to make it ring the changes of a whole day in ten minutes. Half way through noon the poor brute, confused and frantic, gave a last wobbly chime, groaned, and stopped, and somewhere above me a door slammed. I wandered up the stairs, drawing out of the banisters with a moistened finger a thin, piercing wail. There is nothing that cannot be tortured, given a bored child's resourcefulness.

Granny Godkin! Black against the window on the landing hung a grotesque caricature of the old woman, her dusty bombasine evening gown stretched on a spidery frame, my poor mad Mama. The dress hardly covered her shins. Her arms, constricted at the shoulders, dangled crookedly by her sides. Her pale bare wrists were inexplicably pitiable. She stood so, there before that white immensity of snow, her head inclined, listening intently. I stepped toward her slowly through an awful silence, mute, hypnotised, infected with a little bit of her madness. Faint voices crept out from Aunt Martha's room, and a silver jingle of laughter. Mama did not look at me. I doubt if she even realised that I was there. She gave a small grunt of satisfaction, tapped me twice absentmindedly on the shoulder with a fingertip, and skipped swiftly away down the stairs. The voices in Aunt Martha's room fell silent, and after a moment the door opened and my father peered out cautiously. Seeing that it was only me he glared, and received nothing in return but another glare which must have been a disturbing mirror image of his own. Behind his back, in the depths of the room, something lazily stirred, and a muffled voice spoke querulously. Papa retreated and softly closed the door, leaving behind him a woody whiff of cigar smoke.

And later that evening, while I was preparing for a visit to the hayshed to meet Rosie, there floated down from the hushed upper reaches of the house an eerie ululating cry, half laugh, half shriek, a truly terrible sound. I met Papa in the hall. We stared at each other for a moment in trepidation, listening intently.

'Jesus, what now,' he muttered, and plodded up the stairs, his bent black back the very picture of gloom. I followed solemnly after him. Mama stood in the attic among the shallots, still wearing Granny Godkin's gown. She took no notice of us as we entered, but stared into the corner under the roof, where there was a battered tricycle, a dusty bit of cracked mirror leaning drunkenly against the wall, a gutless tennis racket and a black leather trunk with brass studs. Papa sighed.

'What, in the sweet name of Christ, are you at now, Trissy?' he asked, slowly, wearily. Mama did not hear him. She had departed into another world.

'Like black smoke,' she mused, nodding slowly, intrigued. 'Yes, yes.'

Papa took her by the arm. She disengaged herself gently and turned to the door, where she paused and glanced down at my wellingtons, the incongruous badge of my love. Slowly she lifted her eyes to mine, with the faintest of smiles, conspiratorial, tender, and sad.

'Poor boy, poor boy,' she murmured. '*All alone.*'

I stayed in the attic long after they had gone, thinking, I cannot say why, of Rosie waiting for me in a nest of hay. I imagined her very clearly, her fingers blue with cold, her cold lips. All that was finished. Part of my life had fallen away, like a rock into the sea. I do not think I am exaggerating.

THE SNOW MELTED, the earth quickened. Spring came early. In March there was a brief mock summer, strange balmy days, still and close. I would have preferred the toothed winds of other years. Mama steadily journeyed on into the deeps of her new world. There was about her sickness something whimsical and mischievous, a secretive knowing air, almost as if *she* were humouring *us*. She laughed softly under her breath, and smiled hazily, mysteriously past us, clawing a paper napkin asunder under the table, the damp torn pieces falling to the floor like shreds of her own anguish. Some days she would go raging through the house, an uncanny replica of Granny Godkin, others she was a sobbing caricature of her gentle self. There was no denying her madness, and yet, in our hearts, we did try, with desperate nonchalance, to gainsay it. But none of us was really sane, I am convinced of that, none of the Godkins or their kin. Aunt Martha, during our increasingly rare tutorials, was given to sudden silences, unwarranted starts of fright, and often, with eyes narrowed and mouth working tensely, she would question me on my activities on certain and, for me, forgotten days. My indifferent answers provoked in her an excited hum of suspicion, but of what she suspected me I did not know. She fought interminable battles now with Papa over the mysterious terms of his will. Her son too cultivated new peculiarities, skulking in the garden among the bushes, on the stairs at dusk, preoccupied and distant, glancing at me covertly from under his pale brows. I began to wonder if they were all sharing a secret from which I was excluded, and my thoughts turned again and again to my lost sister, of whose existence I was now convinced, but in a detached, unreal way, I cannot explain.

On the feast of Saint Gabriel the Archangel my father laid an unsteady hand on my shoulder and steered me into the library for a little chat, as he called it. He bade me sit on an upright chair in front of his desk while with ponderous solemnity he locked the door and pocketed the key. Then he sat down opposite me with his fists clenched before him, grimaced over a stifled sour belch, and gave me briefly one of his awful icy grins. He was half shot already.

'Well Gabriel?' he began heartily. 'I suppose you know what we're here to talk about? I've dropped enough hints, eh? No? O...O well now.' His eyes slid away from mine and gazed dully past me toward the window. It was a restless bright day, full of wind and misty light. The sight of the flushed spring garden seemed to annoy him. He unclenched his fists and drummed his fingers on the green blotter, regarding me with one eyebrow raised and one eyetooth bared. For Papa, the ideal of a son never fused with my reality. On those rare occasions when he could not avoid acknowledging my existence, it was with a vaguely disconcerted eye, a faintly rueful frown, that he considered me, his little pride and joy.

'Well what I want to say to you Gabriel is, this house...' He waved a hand before him, lifted his eyes to the ceiling, and sat quite still for a moment, frowning. Then he pushed back his chair and wrenched open a drawer, took out a flat leather-covered flask and tipped a shot of brandy into the cap, and hurriedly, almost angrily, threw the liqour down his throat. 'Ach! frightful stuff. Anyway, Gabriel, this house, what with your mother sick, and, well, everything, I've been thinking—and your Aunt Martha thinks so too—that it's not really the place for a growing boy to...grow up, you know? Look, son, what I'm really trying to say, now I'll be honest with you, straight from the shoulder, between men, what I'm saying is...' He was silent once more, and looked at me glassy-eyed, helpless, his mouth moving feebly. Out came the flask again, and this time he left it standing by him, his right-hand man. Eventually, having circled the subject for as long as was possible, he came to the point. I was to be sent away to school.

I did not react at all to this supposedly stunning notion, but sat with my hands folded and waited for him to continue. He was surprised at my calmness, and disappointed too, I think. Did he expect tears and tantrums, a fit on the floor and drumming heels? If he did he knew nothing of his son. He rose heavily and plodded to the window, where he stood looking out, and the fingers of his clasped hands played with each other behind his back.

'Mist is lifting,' he said. 'Be a grand day presently. I remember when I was your age, here. Better times.'

He came back again and sat down with a sigh, pressing his knuckles to his forehead. He took another drink.

'It was easier then to be...for your grandfather to...I mean I was *happy*! I had plenty to occupy me, friends, people used to come here. The parties we had! And then Martha, your Aunt Martha and I were very close, very...close.' He glanced at me swiftly, with a shifty eye. 'We were like pals, great pals. We had grand times, plenty of laughs, parties, all that. Things were better.' He gazed glumly at his hands, shaking his head sorrowfully over the dead past. 'People had more time, it went slower then, there was more...time. Yes. Great pals. And, you see, your Mama is going away too, into a...into a home.'

We were silent. He was getting old, beginning to crack. It was nothing to do with wrinkles or gray hairs, but it was a slackening of an inner fibre, a loosening of grip, his great word, grip. *Keep a grip, boy, just keep a grip and you'll be all right.* One did not need to be strong, only strong enough to keep one's weakness hidden, that was what he meant, I suppose. I watched him there, guzzling cheap brandy, good old Papa. What does one feel for a father? Resentment, disappointment—love? What do they mean, these words? Once I had respected and feared him, captivated by his violence, his arrogance, his pain. Now I only disliked him, found him distasteful. He would not send me away, for I was gone away already. Birchwood was dead. He started up again, like an ancient engine.

'I haven't much advice for you, boy. Always try to play fair. Nobody likes a sneak, you know the kind of chap I mean, a bit of a mama's boy, a cissy, always mooning around the place, always...' He stopped, perhaps realising that it was precisely my type he had described. 'Well anyway, be a man, learn what life is about. Do the right thing! That's what I mean. And you won't go wrong.' He lifted a clenched fist between us and grinned again. I knew what was coming. '*Grip*,' he said softly. 'It's your only man.'

For a moment he was his old self again, agate-eyed, bright-toothed, the tiger of Birchwood, but the moment passed, and he was back to brooding, sighing through his nose, grinding his teeth. He sat sideways at the desk with his legs crossed and one elbow on the blotter, his chin sunk on his breast. The flask was empty. I turned away from him. How gay the garden seemed, how bright, beyond this room with its dead books and dust, its weariness. Michael crossed the lawn, a small distressed figure against the windswept trees. He disappeared behind the glasshouses, going toward the hayshed. Papa stirred. The chair groaned under his heavy thighs.

'Yes, learn what life is about, the hard way, the way we all had to. It's not all poems and roses, take it from me, no, not by a long chalk. I learned, aye. I was like you once, I was, full of dreams. O I was going to do great things, great bloody things, make a mark on the world, yes indeed. I soon learned.'

He stood up, faltered, clapped a hand to the desk to steady himself, and then began to pace up and down behind me, waving his arms excitedly. Bits of white grime gathered at the corners of his mouth.

'No bed of roses, that's for certain. You have to learn that lesson before you go out in the world, because if you don't, take it from me, you'll make a ballocks of it. Look around you, you can start to learn here, anywhere, it doesn't matter a damn. Take a look! Well, what do you see?' Together we considered the room. 'Aye. Aye. That's the way it is all right.'

He flung himself down on the chair again and thrust his face across the desk at me, the veins in his neck straining, his bloodless lips parted, eyes brimming with a passionate sorrow and distress, agonised and mute. For fully a minute we sat so, our noses nearly touching. His fervour slowly drained away, leaving his large grey face with its violet shadows and moist eyes lugubrious and weary. When he spoke his voice was a harsh whisper.

'We get up in the bloody morning, and we go to bed at night, and there's nothing to do. We think we're doing things, making the world sit up and take notice. We give ourselves heartburn, we're so busy running up and down, and all the time, nothing. And we're sick of ourselves. Look into your heart, boy, listen to it. What does it say to you? What does it show? Nothing. And that's what you'll learn is there. Say it after me. *Nothing*. Say it!'

I turned my face away from him again, to the window, to the wide world. I said softly,

'Nothing.'

He relaxed, and withdrew his head, an old tortoise, and contemplated me in silence for a moment, nodding slowly, and then he said, in a tone compounded of a little pride and great disgust,

'You're your father's son, no doubt of that.'

He unlocked the door for me, rattling the key in the lock, and laid his hand awkwardly on my shoulder. The falsity of the gesture made his fingers tremble.

'Get your things together. Josie will fix you up. Train is at eight in the morning. And Gabriel. O, nothing—'

At that word he bit his lip, and suddenly grinned, gaily, guiltily, and hastily retreated, closing the door in my face. I turned, and another hand descended on my shoulder.

IT WAS AUNT MARTHA, very distraught, her hair standing on end, her lips quivering.

'Well?' she snarled, glaring at me accusingly out of her cat's eyes. 'What was all that about? Speak! And where's Michael? You little beast, sneaking around, sticking your nose in. You're a sly little boy, do you know that, do you? I saw you with the blotting paper.' This was a reference to my effort to read the smudges on Papa's green blotter by holding it before a mirror one day after I had overheard talk of his famous will. I thought I had not been observed. It hardly mattered, since all the mirror gave me back were blots turned the right way about but still illegible. Aunt Martha's talons sank deeper into my shoulder. 'Little lord of the manor, you are, smirking there. Young Lord Snot. Well we'll see about that too, let me tell you. I asked you where he is, didn't I, now where *is* he?'

I smiled at her sweetly and said nothing, not a word. I had to admit that this new concern for her son and his whereabouts interested me, but it would have needed more than interest for me to speak of her then. She released me, and with a little gasp of fury turned and strode away down the hall. Later I saw her wandering distracted up and down the lawn, calling Michael's name and wringing her hands. By nightfall he had still not returned and she dragged Papa into the hall to telephone the police.

'But, but,' he spluttered, wriggling in her grasp. He was quite drunk. She propped him against the wall and thrust the phone into his hands, and he mumbled into it, looking at her with pained, injured eyes.

'I can't get through, the lines must be down.' He glowered at the smug black machine. 'The bastards,' he said cryptically.

Aunt Martha began to cry.

'O god O god O god!' she wailed.

Papa bared his teeth.

'Ah for the love of Jesus, Martha, the boy is probably off in a ditch somewhere with some tart. Have a bit of sense, woman. Now listen—'

'Listen! Listen to what? Jesus Christ, you listen. You don't know him, Joe, you don't *know* him. If he brings that crowd here—'

'Ah, shite!' He caught sight of me, and giggled suddenly and said to her, 'There's the one you should be worrying about. *He's* the one.'

Aunt Martha's swollen face collapsed completely, as though a fine lace of supports behind it had crumbled.

'Fifteen years!' she wailed. 'Fifteen years you kept me stuck in that place, no money, no friends, and you only coming when you felt like it. I gave you my life and you ruined it! You broke your word, you cheated us. O god I was a fool. Damn you damn you *damn you*!'

He pushed her out of his way and staggered toward the library, waving his arms as though a cloud of flies were pursuing him. Martha sat down slowly on the chair beside the hatstand and wept into her hands as I had never seen her weep before, for these tears were real. After a while she lifted her head and looked at me with anguish and hatred.

'You,' she said softly. 'O you won, didn't you, you little bastard. I wish to Christ you had never been born.'

I climbed to my room. A low whistle rose from the garden, and when I opened the window and leaned out I saw a dark figure standing below on the lawn. It was Michael. He cupped his hands around his mouth and hissed,

'*They have your sister, Gabriel.*'

I heard him laugh, and he walked backward slowly and disappeared into the trees. I closed the window and sat on the bed for a long time without moving, and then took from the wardrobe a rucksack. Dazed moths staggered out of the folds. I was on my way.

IN THE EARLY HOURS of the morning I was awakened by distant cries and, most incongruous of sounds, the clanging of a bell. A red light danced on the wall above my bed. I lay for a while without stirring, fuddled with sleep. A voice which seemed to be in the room with me said, very calmly, *here it comes*, and the bell banged louder, and there was the rattle of hoofs and the grate of steel-rimmed wheels on gravel. I struggled up and wrapped a blanket around my shoulders. The glasshouses glowed with ruby light. The hayshed was on fire. Rosie–the bitch!

I do not see the stairs, but I recall the shock of cold tiles under my bare feet when I reached the hall. The front door was open back to the wall, and there Mama and Aunt Martha stood confronting each other, very strange, very still, like stone figures guarding the doorway. They were both fully dressed, and I realised immediately that I had found them at the end of a long and bitter quarrel. Mama was smiling. That smile.

'Dear Martha,' she said, 'I've told you, he's in the shed down there.'

Aunt Martha bared her teeth.

'Mad bitch,' she said softly. The words slipped from her lips like a silken red ribbon of hatred. She swept out to the porch, where she halted and stared back at us over her shoulder with an impossibly melodramatic look, eyes smouldering and nostrils flared. She disappeared. Mama touched my cheek. Behind her there was wind, a frozen moon, black trees. Suddenly I had an irrational desire to strike her. Instead I pushed her aside and ran down the steps, across the garden. The blanket clutched at my legs, and I must have fallen more than once, for in the morning my knees were crusted with dried blood and bits of grit. The fire wagon was parked at the corner of the garden, its two black horses stamping the grass uneasily and rolling their eyes. Dim figures were busy in the glass-houses, and a white canvas hose, swelling and writhing like a stranded eel, crawled through a smashed frame and down the path toward the rear of the house, where I followed it.

The shed was a glorious sight. Enormous scarlet flames poured through the door and the windows, lighting with an evil glow the underside of the tumbling pall of black smoke above the roof. In the open yard squat firemen in outsize uniforms were running up and down and shouting. There seemed to be a horde of them. Two stalwarts grappled valiantly with the gasping hose and sprayed a stream of water on the cobbles, the empty sties, even on the burning shed, and once on the figure of Aunt Martha, a tragic queen, standing below the flames with her arms flung wide, her face livid in the glare. The fire roared like a wounded animal, but it could not drown out her piercing cry.

'*Michael!*'

She dropped her arms and set off toward the shed with an odd broken stride, her hands flapping. Josie and a fireman made a lunge at her and missed, and the fireman darted after her, tapped her on the shoulder, and then, beaten by the heat, turned and scampered back to his mates. I thought that he giggled, like a child playing tig. It was an extraordinary moment, in which it seemed that the whole yard was about to erupt into guffaws.

Aunt Martha halted outside the burning doorway, and remained there, apparently at a loss, for a very long time, and Papa, looming up behind me like a huge pale spider in his long woolly underwear, gave a grunt of astonishment as she lifted her arm to brush the sweat from her forehead with a languid, lazy, stylised gesture of weariness. Acting still! Her dress burst into flames then, and she trotted on through the door. Her wild, ululating cry was the perfect counterpart of her rippling figure as it drifted, so it seemed, slowly, dreamily, wrapped in an aureole of light, into the furnace. Papa opened his mouth and bawled, angrily, terribly, and covered his face with his hands, and in that theatrical pose I left him, as a fireman, no doubt acting out some cherished notion of heroism, grabbed me up out of the path of a non-existent danger and went pounding off around the house to the front door, where Mama still stood, still smiling placidly.

DOWN IN THE GLOOM of the kitchen Josie fed me bread and butter and bruised bananas and scalding tea. A naked bulb, like a drop of bright yellow fat, burned above the table where my stout-hearted fireman, balancing his helmet on his knee, sat with his nose in a steaming mug. Each time I looked at him he winked slyly, as though we were conspirators. Perhaps we were? Josie, wrapped in a shapeless quilted dressing gown which had once been Granny Godkin's, stood silently by the stove stirring and stirring something in a huge saucepan. Her hair stood upright on her head, grey spikes and springs. I think she was asleep on her feet. Outside in the darkness a lone bird sang, foolishly welcoming the false dawn. Mama brought down my clothes and I dressed on the warm tiles beside the stove. Josie grinned at me sleepily. I felt like a little child again. We heard the fire wagon depart, and at the sound my rescuer started up in alarm. His helmet fell to the floor and rolled about drunkenly. He retrieved it quickly and sat down again, grinning sheepishly, and ever after that morning the angel of death has been for me a fat celestial fireman with a permanent wink and a helmet perilously balanced over one ear. Mama, with her fingers pressed to her cheek, sat by the table and watched me dressing.

'You never cried,' she mused, idly. 'Never once, did you?' I shook my head. She took me in her arms and kissed me tenderly. She had a smell, of milk, of hair, of violets, the smell of madness. 'My Gabriel.'

Once, when I was very young, I had this strange experience. I was standing, I remember, by the french windows in the library looking out into a garden full of butterflies and summer, as gardens always seem to be when we are very young. I thought to open the windows and walk out there, into the sunlight, but with my fingers on the handle I hesitated, for no reason, and for an instant only, and then I went out. But I was followed by a terrifying notion that there was ahead of me, as far ahead as the duration of that momentary hesitation, a phantom of myself who mimicked my every movement precisely, but in another world, another time. That same conviction, but this time profounder and more terrible, was with me as I slipped out of the house at first light. It was a gauzy green dawn, damp and bright. The birds, my faithful friends! There were lavender shadows under the trees. The hayshed still smouldered, a black sore in the midst of spring's tempestuous greenery. I caught a glimpse of Papa down there, wandering in the ruins, dazed and lost. I left him there and went down the drive. Birchwood dwindled behind me. Far along the road the shimmering roofs of the town were visible, with here and there a little plume of ashblue smoke. I thought about Michael. Many things puzzled me. Why had Aunt Martha died? Did Rosie set fire to the shed in revenge for my abandoning her? Where was Michael? And my sister? All these questions, and many more. I longed for answers. O but no, I did not really long. They could wait, for another time.

PART II

Air and Angels

IT WAS STILL EARLY when I reached the town. The sunlight was bluish, laden with soft dust. More like summer really than spring, except for that sensation of pins and needles in the air. The townsfolk were abed, but stirring, I could hear them. I was stared at by dogs, by sleepy cats with cloudy green poison in their eyes. I have always felt a friend to dumb creatures. A milk cart creaked down the narrow main street, the horse with its tail arched dropping a trail of steaming brown pats like hoofs come undone. The milkman wore trousers made from flourbags. He landed a spit between my feet. Admirable aim.

I sat on the steps below a fragment of an ancient rampart. The barracks with its barred windows faced me across the road. To my left was the priory, with broken tombstones, a tower and a green bronze bell. Monks were slaughtered there by Cromwell. Some hard thing struck me on the spine. It was the toe of a boot. He stood behind and above me on the steps with the sun at his back, his hands on his hips. He wore a dark-green frock-coat with black and gold frogging, tight white duck trousers, stout black boots and gaiters laced to the knee. On his square head a cocked hat sat, with a flowing ostrich plume in the band. A white wirebrush moustache bristled under his granite nose. The voice when he spoke was like a distant cannonade.

'Richard FitzGilbert de Clare, Earl of Pembroke, stood there.' He eyed me distastefully, pointing at the spot where I sat. 'Strong-bow himself, that was, on them very steps! Now bugger off.'

A most extraordinary fellow. What had I done to merit his displeasure? And the outfit! Extraordinary. I retreated under that fierce blue stare and from a safe distance threw a stone at him. He shook his fist.

'*Whelp!*'

I wandered idly up through the town. A joybell chimed, its ponderous music dancing on the morning air. A band somewhere began to clear its brassy throats. Around me in the narrow crooked streets a concourse swelled. There were droves of children, boys in white shirts and sashes, and little girls very pretty in pale-blue dresses wearing flowers in their hair. Fat babies in the arms of their fat mothers hung out of upstairs windows. Shawled crones gathered in gaggles here and there, shuffling their black boots. The menfolk leaned on their blackthorn sticks, their ankles crossed, big hardfaced fellows with knobbly hands and battered tall hats. A priest with a red bullneck and cropped carroty hair, his cassock swinging, strode up and down barking orders, vigorously cuffing little boys. A dogfight broke out, fangs and fur everywhere, foam flying. The band with a discordant blast of music wheeled into view. Strongbow and a group of his peers marched smartly out of a sidestreet, their ostrich feathers dipping. It was the feast of Our Lady of the Harbour. There was to be a procession.

On the footpath near me I noticed a raffish pair, a rednosed portly old man in a tight black suit and an odd-looking hat perched on a head of grizzled curls, and a fat woman with lank black hair and a broad flat yellowish face. They watched the milling crowd with amiable though faintly derisive smiles. There was about them something curious, an air, I could not quite identify it, but certainly they were not of the town. And there were others too, I amused myself by picking them out from the crowd, a young man with a dark brow and hot black eyes, two strange pale girls, a spare stringy man with big ears, all of them ignoring each other yet all joined by an invisible bond. The most outlandish of the lot were the two blonde children, androgynous, identical, exquisite, who, with their arms linked and their heads together, stood sniggering at Strongbow and his men. They wore sandals and shorts and yellow tunics with tight gold collars. Their lips and cheeks were painted, their eyebrows drawn in black. When I looked again for the pair who had been beside me, they were gone. On a broken-down wooden gate near where they had stood a bright red poster was pinned.

PROSPERO'S MAGIC CIRCUS
by apointment to the
CROWNED HEADS OF EUROPE

magicians actors
acrobats clowns
wild beasts

THRILLS!
SPILLS!
EXCITEMENT!

Admission 6d
CHILDREN 2d

for one week only

'WE WERE AMUSED'

HRH
The Queen

The others too were gone, but they too had left posters behind them, pinned to doors, stuck on windows, wrapped around lampposts. This bright spoor I followed. It led me down to the harbour, along the quay, a merry chase, until at last, in a field outside the town, I spied their horsedrawn caravans parked beside a big red tent. The caravans were garish ramshackle affairs daubed with rainbows of peeling paint, with stovepipe chimneys and poky little windows and halfdoors at the front. Grasses and moss, even a primrose or two, sprouted between the warped boards of the barrel-shaped roofs. The horses, starved bony brutes, stood about the field with drooping heads, spancelled, apparently asleep. The tent was crooked, and sagged ominously. A woman unseen began to sing. That sad song, rising through the still spring morning, called to me. I entered the field. The old boy with the odd hat sat sprawled on the steps at the rear of one of the caravans with his hands clasped on his big belly and his rapt smiling face turned upward toward the open door, from whence the singing came. It stopped abruptly, and I stepped forward.

'Pardon me, sir. Are you Mr Prospero?'

The old man started and peered at me over his shoulder. Behind him, in the gloom of the doorway, one of the pale girls, the singer, was sitting on a chair, silent now, pulling a daisy asunder with her long glittering nails.

'Eh?' the old man grunted. He had plump pink lips and small bright blue eyes, a hooked nose. I remember his boots, worn thin and wrinkled like black paper.

'Are you—?'

'I am not,' he answered cheerfully. 'Fuck off now.'

The pale girl spoke briefly in a low voice. He looked up at her, frowned, and turned to me again.

'Why, I believe you're right, my dear,' he murmured. 'Well well.' He struggled up from his sprawling position, but did not rise, and leaned forward to scrutinise my face, my clothes, and craned his neck and peered at the pack on my back. 'A travelling man, I perceive. Tell me, boy, what is your name?'

'Gabriel, sir.'

'Gabriel Sir?'

'No sir, Godkin. Gabriel Godkin.'

He raised his eyebrows and pursed his lips.

'Godkin, eh? Well now, that's a fine name to have, a fine old name. And tell me this now, Gabriel Godkin, who sent you here?' I did not answer. 'And you come from where?' Again, no answer. My silence seemed to satisfy him. He sat and beamed at me with his plump hands resting on his knees. Behind him the girl stirred and sighed. Her face was wide at the eyes, white, curiously boneless. She was not pretty, I would not say pretty, but striking, certainly, with those eyes, the straw-coloured hair, that trancelike calm. The old boy chuckled softly and glanced up at her.

'He wants to see Prospero, did you hear? Did you hear that?' He turned to me once again, shaking his head, still beaming. *Nobody sees Prospero*. Why, I don't recall that I ever saw him myself! How about that now. You don't say much, do you, Gabriel Godkin? Still, there are worse faults, worse faults.' He slapped his knees and stood up, hoisted up his trousers, tugged at his tight waistcoat. In spite of his bulk and the untidiness it entailed he possessed a certain elegance. We shook hands solemnly.

'I am Silas,' he said. 'Come along with me now.'

I followed him down the line of caravans to the largest of them, painted black, and there, with another smile, in silence, he led me up the steps. They were all in there, perched on stools, reclining on the narrow bunks, standing idly about, the youth with the hot eyes, the fat woman, golden children, all. There was a great silence, and a smell of boiled tea. At my back the pale girl entered quietly. She went and stood by her twin, who was her double except for her ravenblack hair. No one said a word, but they all smiled, a symphony of strange smiles around me. Silas rubbed his hands.

'Well here we are,' he said. 'Allow me to present—this is Angel, and Mario there, young Justin and Juliette.' The painted children bowed and tittered. 'And the baba under the table, little Sophie. Come out and say howdedoo, baba. Shy, are you? This is Magnus, and Sybil here, and last, but ah! the very best, my darling girls, Ada, Ida.' He laid a hand on my shoulder and took a deep breath. 'Children, this is Gabriel Godkin.'

I was confused. The names all slipped away from the faces, into a jumble. The tall slender woman with flame-red hair and agate eyes, Sybil it was, turned her face from the window and looked at me briefly, coldly. Still no one spoke, but some smiled. I felt excitement and unease. It seemed to me that I was being made to undergo a test, or play in a game the rules of which I did not know. Silas put his hands in his pockets and chuckled again, and all at once I recognised the nature of the bond between them. Laughter! O wicked, mind you, and vicious perhaps, but laughter for all that. And now I laughed too, but, like theirs, my laughter made no sound, no sound at all.

SILAS TOOK ME next on a tour of his collapsible kingdom. Now strictly speaking it was not a circus at all, but a kind of travelling theatre. Here was no big top strung with a filigree of tightropes and gleaming trapeze bars, but a long rectangular tent with benches and a stage, the latter an awkward hinged affair which took a workparty of four an hour to dismantle. The canvas roof above us, cooking slowly in the sun, gave off a smell of sweat and glue. I felt obscurely betrayed. There were worse disappointments in store. Out behind the tent we found the wild beasts promised by the poster, a melancholy tubercular grey monkey in a birdcage, and a motheaten tiger lying motionless behind bamboo bars on a trailer. The monkey bared his yellow teeth and turned contemptuously away from us, displaying his skinned purplish backside. I peered into the tiger's glassy yellow eye and ventured to enquire if it was alive. Silas laughed.

'Stuffed!' he cried, greatly tickled. 'Yet very lifelike, would you not say? Fearsome. Ha!' He clasped his hands on the shelf of his big belly and beamed at me, not without fondness, amused by my chagrin. 'It is *real*, you know, Gabriel. They find it quite convincing.'

They were the folk who paid to look upon these wonders. There was both mockery and reverence in the way he spoke the word. People believed the shoddy dreams he sold them! The fact filled him with awe.

'You see, my boy, they pay to gape at our stuffed friend here, to make faces at Albert the monkey, to watch us capering about the stage, they *pay*, mark you, and their pennies work like magic wands, transforming all they buy.'

We sat down side by side on the shaft of the trailer. He took from his waistcoat pocket a short black pipe and stuck it between his teeth, folded his arms and gazed at the blue hills away behind the town. I watched him suspiciously, with the uneasy feeling that he was making fun of me. He was an odd old man. I liked him. The sun, still low, was in our faces, and now I saw a figure approach out of a mist of light, skimming down the path by the caravans, a tiny figure on a threewheeled cycle. At first I thought it must be Prospero, and I stared at Silas. He said nothing. The little man pulled up before us and put one sharp shoe to the ground. He had a big square head and enormous hands. His black eyebrows and his hair were as smooth as fur. He wore a neat grey suit tightly buttoned. A red scarf was knotted at his throat. He was less than four feet tall.

'Well well,' said Silas, by way of greeting. 'There you are.'

The little man stepped down from his cycle, tugged the wrinkles out of his jacket deftly with finger and thumb, and gravely bowed.

'Silas, my friend, how are you? And... ?'

'This is Gabriel.'

He shook my hand.

'The name is Rainbird,' he said loftily, as though presenting to me something of inestimable value. We made room for him on the shaft and he settled himself daintily between us, clasping his mighty hands in his lap. Silas looked at him over his pipe and asked,

'Well, any news?'

Rainbird squirmed, feigning a delicious horror.

'What a day, O! what a day. Would you believe it, I was knocked off my bike. Just look at my things.' There were a few faint mudstains on his jacket and his shoes were damp. 'A child it was, a little girl, no higher than that. I could have slapped her face, I really could. And what's so funny, may I ask?' Silas was chuckling. He turned his laughter into a cough and waved his hands apologetically. Rainbird sniffed. 'I see nothing funny, I'm sure.'

He turned his attention to me and looked me up and down with a calm appraising gaze, and, still with his odd eye upon me, said to Silas,

'Not much doing in these parts. Tenant farms, mostly. A village or two. They say the gentry are trigger-happy. Go north is our best bet.'

Silas nodded, paying scant attention to this information. He said to me,

'Rainbird is our scout.'

The little man glared at him.

'O that's all,' he said, with heavy sarcasm. 'Our *scout*. Nothing more.'

Silas grinned, still gazing away toward the hills.

'Does a couple of tricks too, for the show.'

'Tricks! Well!' cried Rainbird. He ruminated darkly for a while, then shrugged and turned to me again. 'Well Gabriel? Another hopeful, I suppose?'

'Yes sir.'

'Running away from home, are you?'

'Yes sir.'

'Aha, I thought so.'

'Sir, the girl, the one who knocked you off your bike...?'

Although Silas did not stir, or look at me, I fancied that his delicate almost pointed ears quivered. I was sorry at once that I had spoken, and cursed myself inwardly for my incontinence. Had I not vowed that I would proceed upon my quest in silence cunningly? Now here I was, blurting out my heart's secrets, with no going back. Rainbird was examining me with a new interest, waiting for me to finish my question. When he saw that I would not, he said,

'She was some child, I don't know. Why?'

Silas took the pipe out of his mouth and peered into the bowl, poked at the dottle with the nail of his little finger, clamped the pipe between his teeth again, gave it a couple of experimental puffs and put a match to it. He was waiting for me to proceed, and a perfect blue smoke ring, hovering above his head, seemed somehow to betray, unsuspected by himself, the very shape of his interest. Rainbird glanced inquiringly from one of us to the other. I found to my surprise that I had begun to enjoy my position at the centre of attention.

'Well, I'm searching for someone, you see,' I said, and added, faintly, 'a girl.'

Rainbird's mouth formed a little circle, and he said,

'Oo, are you now, indeed?'

'Yes. My sister.' They looked at each other and nodded slowly, apparently much impressed. 'My twin,' I said, quite reckless now. 'She was stolen—'

'By fairies?' Rainbird asked innocently.

'No no. I never knew her, you see, I mean I don't remember her, but I'm sure...that is I...'

I stopped, and looked at them suspiciously. They were altogether too solemn. Silas put a florid red handkerchief to his nose and blew a trumpet blast. Rainbird's nostrils quivered peculiarly.

'And her name?' he asked.

'I—I don't know.'

'O? And what does she look like?'

Silas nudged him.

'He doesn't know that either, I'll bet.'

They brooded for a moment, and Rainbird drew a deep breath and said gravely,

'Why then you have plenty of scope, haven't you?'

Silas gave a great sneeze of laughter, and Rainbird hugged his knees, pleased as punch with his joke. Their merriment made the shaft tremble under us. I could not understand it. Granted, my story had sounded silly, but why did they find it so screamingly funny? Once again I felt, as I had felt in the caravan earlier, that I was the only one who was ignorant of the rules of their game.

'*Plenty of scope!*' Rainbird squeaked, beside himself, and slapped Silas on the back. The old man began to cough uproariously. After a while their hilarity subsided, and Rainbird happily swung his little legs. I said icily,

'I have a picture of her, you know.'

Silas gave me a curious glance.

'I'm sure you have,' he murmured, and it was impossible to tell from his tone whether he believed me or was being sarcastic. Without another word I strode away from them, to the black caravan under the steps of which I had left my pack. The golden children, Justin and Juliette, leaned out over the halfdoor and watched me eagerly as I rummaged through my things and brought out the small framed photograph. I hurried back the way I had come, and met Rainbird and Silas strolling with the cycle between them. Silas took the picture from me, and glanced at it and handed it to Rainbird, who winked.

'She's a dandy,' he said, and sniggered.

Silas laid his hand on my head and smiled at me benignly.

'Come along,' he said, 'come along, Sir Smile.'

THAT NIGHT, as the ramshackle dream of the Magic Circus unfolded, I sat with damp hands and dancing heart in the centre of the third bench from the front, from whence in a little while Silas would pluck me out into the glare and glitter of my new career. The packed audience vibrated, sweating with excitement, their faces lit by the flickering glow from the oil lamps on the stage, where Magnus of the big ears sat on a stool squeezing rollicking tunes out of a wheezy accordion. We did our best to sing along with him, but no one knew the words, and there rose from the benches a drone of moans and mumbles in the midst of which I feared my own stagefright was audible, a piercing hum. At last, with a last flourish on the squeezebox, Magnus withdrew, and to the accompaniment of a roll on an unseen bodhran Silas sauntered out of the wings with his arms hieratically lifted. He welcomed the patrons, he sketched the delights the evening held in store. His hat was as black as a raven's wing.

Exit Silas right, bowing low, and enter left Mario the juggler, his black eyebrows arched, who filled the stage with glittering wheels and flashing spokes of light. His splendid scowl never faltered though the whirling rings got tangled on his wrists and the indian clubs cracked together like skulls, and his hot eyes only burned more fiercely the more hopelessly his act went askew. Next came Rainbird in a wizard's cloak, and a pointed paper hat festooned with silver stars which provoked some hilarity among the young bucks at the back of the tent. He conjured billiard balls out of the air, transformed a cane into a silk scarf. A white mouse escaped from a hidden pocket in his cloak.

The pale twins, Ada and Ida, barefoot, swathed in veils, danced a solemn pavane to the accompaniment of a tune from Mario's tin whistle. The audience sat rapt, heedless of the incongruous bump of bare heels on the boards. The dance ended and the girls drooped sinuously into the wings, fluttering their pale fingers. A roar went up. The men whistled and stamped their feet, the women bravely smiled, but in a moment all were silent as Magnus tumbled head over heel across the stage and leapt to his feet before us, grinning. He wore huge checked trousers, sagging braces, outsize frock coat, false bald skull, a cherry nose.

'*I say I say I say...*'

We had Mario again, in a new outfit, heaving Justin and Juliette about the stage in a display of acrobatics. They raised a storm of dust. Flamehaired Sybil, with Magnus and Mario disguised in hunting pink, played a scene from a popular melodrama. Eyes flashed, riding crops whistled.

'*Aubrey, that cad deserves a thrashing !*'

I had begun to think that my moment would never come, but at last the bodhran rolled again and Silas appeared in a dented top hat and white gloves, and a frock coat which still bore some dusty traces of its first appearance on the back of Magnus the clown. He was followed by Justin and Juliette carrying between them a mysterious something hidden under a black cloth. They set it down on a table in the centre of the stage. Silas doffed his hat, peeled off his gloves and laid them on the table. He adjusted the pin in his cravat. The audience shifted its backside restlessly.

'*Who knows,*' Silas cried, turning suddenly and glaring down upon us, 'who knows the power of the will, ah, my friends, the strength and weakness of the mind ?'

We pondered the question while he pulled on his gloves again, put on his hat. He advanced to the edge of the stage.

'Ladies and gentlemen,' he said quietly, 'I am the keeper of dark powers, bestowed upon me by the gipsies of Persia. The druids of old knew nothing of which I do not know, the secrets of the alchemists are my secrets. I am Silas, to whom the world's will is as a twig, to be snapped—like that!'

He clicked his fingers, and behind him the golden children whipped away the black cloth and revealed Albert the monkey sitting in his cage with his arms folded and his black lips drawn back. The audience gasped. Albert scratched his belly. Silas smiled faintly.

'My assistant,' he said, and opened the door of the cage. Albert peered up at him inquiringly, shrugged, and clambered out and perched on a corner of the table. Silas closed his eyes and put his hand upon the creature's bald head, stood motionless for a moment and suddenly cried out, staggered, regained his balance, and roared,

'Now his power is mine, will strengthen mine, his very soul has entered me. Look at him, he is empty.' Albert indeed seemed drained, crouched there gaping. 'Only when I have finished here will I give him back his substance, only then—'

Only then Albert's wicked sense of humour got the better of him. He roused himself out of his torpor and sprang on Silas's back and knocked his hat off, jumped down and scampered around the stage, shrieking and chattering, with Justin and Juliette after him. There was pandemonium. The audience was beside itself with glee.

'*Hooray!*'

'A banana, give him a banana.'

'Peg something at him.'

'Aye, peg your man!'

'Wait! He have him.'

'Begob he have him right enough.'

'*Ahh...!*'

Justin lay on the boards and carefully drew out from under him the dazed monkey, and, clutching the brute between them, the children brought him before Silas.

'Ah, wretched animal! Thought you could escape, did you? Thought you could break my power? Here, hold his head, hold him now.' Again he clasped that grey skull in his fist, again he cried out. 'Now! Now, take him away. Go!'

They thrust poor Albert into his cage and swept him off, and Silas turned to us again.

'And now, ladies and gentlemen, I call on you for a volunteer.' My cue! 'Who will test his will against mine? Who among you will risk a journey into the unknown depths of his own soul?' I leapt to my feet and waved my arms, speechless with excitement. Silas beamed at me. At the other side of the hall two or three strapping fellows stood up, grinning foolishly and scratching their heads. Silas adroitly ignored them, and they sat down again abruptly. 'Come up, brave lad, come, this way. Look friends, a beardless youth. And your name?'

All was noise and light up here, another world. Silas prodded me and roared, so it seemed, into my face.

'*Name!*'

'Gab—' I began, and was prodded again.

'What's that? Speak up, boy, don't be afraid.'

'Johann Livelb, sir,' I said, but my voice did not work, and I had to repeat that outlandish alias which Silas had found for me god knows where.

'Well well, a foreigner, eh? Tell me, Johann, would you say that you have a strong will, eh?'

'I don't know, sir—I mean yes. Sir.'

'Yes. Good. Stronger than a monkey's, would you say?'

'Yes.'

Laughter.

'Stronger than mine, would you say?'

I opened my mouth and closed it again. I could not remember the answer, and when I searched in my poor frantic conciousness for the other answers I realised that I could not remember them either. All those lines, so carefully rehearsed, gone! Silas saw that I was lost, and bared his teeth at me. Justin brought out a three-legged stool and I was thrust down upon it. Silas took out his watch, a gold repeater, and dangled it before me on its chain.

'Attend me now, boy, put all your attention upon me, your very soul.' He swung the watch slowly. 'You begin to feel drowsy. Come, you cannot resist me. Ah, sleep comes…sleep…*sleep*…' He pocketed the watch and glanced at the audience. 'See,' he whispered, 'see, he sleeps, he is mine. Boy! Speak!'

He watched me apprehensively as I stood up with my eyes half-closed, my arms hanging limp by my sides. One phrase from all that was lost came back to me.

'*Master, I am your slave, do with me what you could.*'

He winked at me, and turned with a triumphant smile to face the surge of applause.

'Ladies and gentlemen, what shall I have him do, my slave?' He crooked a finger at me and brought me to his side, and for my ears only hissed, '*Would*, not could, you clown.' He was a hard master.

I was made to crow like a cock, crawl like a snake, swim on dry land, leap from the stool with my arms flapping. I sang a song. I danced. The audience roared. Never had I felt such freedom, I cannot explain. Silas snapped his fingers at last and I was sent back to my seat. A great sigh filled the tent. The cast came back on stage to take their bows. I had no regrets at not being in their midst, for there on the bench among the crowd I was a magic creature, a unicorn. Silas laid aside his hat and gloves.

'Gentles, gentles, our revels now are ended...'

IT WAS STRANGE, that so easy deception of so many. I say deception, but that is not it, not exactly. They wished to be deceived, they conspired with us in our fantasies. Silas's act hardly varied all that week—except that Albert more or less behaved himself and I conquered my stagefright—yet those who returned night after night, and they formed more than half of every audience, gazed at his antics with happy enthusiasm as though for the first time. Indeed, toward the end, there appeared in some of those faces a smug proprietary look—*they* knew what was coming next. It was a game that we played, enchanters and enchanted, tossing a bright golden ball back and forth across the footlights, a game that meant nothing, was a wisp of smoke, and yet, and yet, on the tight steel cord of their careful lives we struck a dark rapturous note that left their tidy town tingling behind us.

Tingling too were our players when the lights were doused, and the dreamers straggled home to their second sleep. We all crowded into the cramped dressing-room tent behind the stage, laughing, shouting, falling over each other, knocking over candles, our nerves aquiver, seized by a manic gaiety which sprang from we knew not where, bubbled up through our blood and pop! burst as the greasepaint fell like scales from our eyes. Then one by one, sober now, we crossed the dark field to the black caravan where Angel waited for us with potato soup and bread and huge pots of tea. Most of the night we spent there, conversing idly, while the solitary paraffin lamp burned down. The children dozed, the pale twins sang in soft reedy undertones, and Silas sat in his high rocking chair and smiled down on us all through wreaths of pipesmoke. That was the time I liked best, huddled with my arms around my knees in a dim corner of that smelly warm caravan, drowsy and at ease, the green scent of grass coming up through the floorboards, one trembling star hanging in a corner of the window, and the great night all around me, stretching away across fields and woods and shining marsh pools, all that darkness, that silence.

In those nights they spoke of old times, better times, told fabulous tales, dreamt up new dreams. They never mentioned Prospero. When I asked about him they fell silent, and examined their fingernails, and Magnus, his lugubrious lopsided grin hanging in the gloom, said softly,

'That prosperous fellow!'

So Prospero became for me a mystery bound up with my quest. I liked to imagine him as a tiny withered old man with skin like wrinkled brown paper, sparrow hands, a big hat, a cloak, a crooked stick, pale piercing eyes, always before me, like a black spider, his bent back, the tapping stick, leading me ever on into a mysterious white landscape. I knew that picture was all wrong, but it sufficed. Like our audiences, I also wanted to dream. I knew too that my quest, mocked and laughed at, was fantasy, but I clung to it fiercely, unwilling to betray myself, for if I could not be a knight errant I would not be anything.

Sometimes I had the uncanny feeling that the circus had been expecting me. How else explain my calm reception, that eerie introduction, the silence and the silent laughter? This question I considered through many a long night, and went out in the morning determined to have an answer, only to be disappointed by their impenetrable diffidence. They were loath to speak of themselves, and it took me a long tedious time to assemble even the outlines of their stories. It is true that I was accepted at once into the life of the circus, but I never felt that I belonged completely in their midst, as though the covenant by which they were bound to care for me demanded nothing beyond essentials. Was the cruelty of the golden children a shade crueller when turned on me? Did Sybil's anger have a keener edge when I came under its cuts?

My first difficulty was to unravel the threads of their relationships. For instance I imagined from the start, when they first appeared beside me in the town, that Angel and Silas were husband and wife. I was wrong, I soon discovered that, but what I did not discover for a very long time, for weeks, was that Sybil was his mate. Sybil of the flaming hair, the icy green eyes, Sybil the austere! I was astonished, and at first repulsed. How could this proud patrician creature allow that old goat to share her bed, her secrets, to paw her gleaming limbs? Sybil, with her cold beauty, her impassioned rages, was a vibrant and untouchable mystery, whereas Silas was just old Tosspot, barrel-arsed, wheezy, a laughable codger. Later, when I recognised Sybil's true nature, a bitter brew of spite and pettiness, I had to wonder how Silas, not so simple after all, could tolerate *her*. The answer was that she was his odd notion of beauty made flesh, beauty which was an inexaustible source of both wonder and amusement. One day I found her in their caravan fighting with Angel, screaming, foaming at the mouth. It was no uncommon thing, for Angel took a sweet delight in baiting her. Silas sat by the table with his legs crossed, his thumbs in his waistcoat, beaming at them as if to say, *look, look, is she not exquisite, my Sybil?—and such a fool!*

The pleasure he derived from his wife was intellectual in the main, while his baser longings were directed elsewhere. Once, merrily drunk on poteen, he confided to Rainbird and me his dream, which was to dwell in idyllic concupiscence, his word, with not one but both of the twins, Ada and her dark sister Ida. 'To have them, one on each side of me, in the buff, their tits in my ears, ah, what a thing that would be!' The girls were utterly indifferent to his attentions, but their indifference, he insisted, only goaded him into wilder transports of desire. I could never take seriously this farcical longing, partly for the reason that Silas himself regarded it as a perplexing but funny foible of his old age, and partly because, ironically, he was teaching me in his subtle way to take nothing seriously, or perhaps a better word is solemnly.

The most astonishing discovery of all that I made was that Justin and Juliette, those spiteful sprites, were the product of that union between Silas and Sybil. Yes! I confess I found it impossible to believe at first, and, when he told me, I searched Magnus's face for the twitch that would betray the joke, but it was no joke. I looked at the children with new eyes. They were an uncanny, disturbing couple. In spite of their difference in gender, which was minimal anyway, they were doubles in body and spirit, a beautiful two-headed monster, wicked, destructive, unfailingly gay. Magnus merged them into a single entity which he called Justinette. He had the right idea. I was afraid of them.

Magnus was a born clown. He had a long wedge-shaped head topped with a flat mat of furry fair hair. His thin blue-veined nose, with a knob at the tip, was almost painful to look at in its austerity, and his pale moist eyes, peering out through concentric circles of tired brownish flesh, seemed permanently on the point of over-flowing with a flood of tears. That long sinewy frame, the mournful grin, provoked immediately in an audience the kind of laughter on which jesters thrive, that uproarious hee-haw with a seed of misgiving lodged at its root. He kept us entertained through all our trials except one, perched on his stool with his hands on his bony knees, spinning his elegant tales.

Our last night in the town was wet and wild. Sabres of black rain swept across the sodden field, the wind keened in the guy ropes of the tent. The show was a washout, and the audience, what there was of it, demanded its money back. We huddled in the caravan around the glowing stove, coughing as the smoke came billowing back down the chimney. Even Angel's stewed tea, strong enough to trot a mouse on, as Silas observed, could not revive our spirits, and we sat wrapped in a cocoon of melancholy until Magnus took out his harmonica and played a jig, always the prelude to a yarn.

'Did I ever tell you,' he began, smacking the harmonica on his palm and considering the ceiling with a frown, 'about the Exploding Coffin?'

We snuggled closer to the stove and wrapped our hands around our teamugs. For all the smoke and the draughts, there is nothing on a stormy night so cosy as a caravan. Magnus's droll voice cast a spell about us and drew us out of our dejection, and when I think of him now I realise that of all the creatures I have lost I miss most his valiant and fastidious spirit. Ah Magnus, my friend.

SILAS LOVED the pale twins, and they loved Mario, but Mario's only love was his left hand. He explained his passion to me the day we left the town behind. I rode beside him on the last caravan, which at night I shared with him. It was a gleaming morning, washed clean by the storm in the night. Mario wore his black britches and a loose white shirt. A yellow scarf was knotted tightly around his slender neck. He cut a romantic figure there, with his bandit's black eyes and his angry mouth. In his lap sat Sophie the baby, a solemn watchful child with curly hair.

'I fuckada woman one time, right?' he said, chopping the air with the edge of his hand. 'One time, no more, then she'sa mine, see? You know what I mean? I got her in my head, alla them in here'—he tapped his forehead—'and when I wanta the *real* woman, who do everything, you know? I justa think about one and—ratta tat *tat*! See?'

He laughed. Mario's laugh was something to hear, a sharp humourless snicker like the sound of something chipping nicks out of glass. The baby looked up at him with her saucer eyes. He tickled her fondly. On one of his specimen-gathering expeditions he had, to his intense surprise, fathered Sophie on blonde Ada. Delight, yes. His daughter was the one thing which could strike through his congenital beastliness and touch a faint and otherwise concealed vein of tenderness in him. That such a bright warm toy could spring unbidden out of that joyless gallop, there was something to wonder at. Ada's feelings, on the other hand, were quite untouched. She carried her load for as brief a time as possible before she spat out the brat and thrust it on Mario, and forgot about it.

The twins were alike only in appearance. Spiritually they were as different as dark and light. Ada, for all her golden beauty, was one of Mario's kind, sullen, given to incoherent rages, dark laughter, careless cruelty, yet one who, with her wanton ways, displayed a certain vicious splendour. She was a voracious eater. While the rest of us made do with potatoes and bread in various ingenious combinations, she always managed to find meat or fruit, some delicacy, supplied mostly by Magnus, who had a way with snares and things, and who also, I suspect, nursed a secret longing for Ada's wild flesh. Lolling with that negligent grace on her bunk, she would tear in her small white teeth the roasted leg of a rabbit, or a salmon's tender pink flank, greedy, and at the same time indifferent. Her life she lived at the tips of her five senses, and yet if one were foolish enough to strike one's will against hers there came back immediately a startling clang, for there was steel at her centre.

Ida, now, ah, our gentle Ida. She came to us when we stopped at noon, bringing our food, and sat with Sophie on the grass at the side of the road while we ate. The girl and the baby watched us with the same intent gaze, as though they were witnessing the celebration of some outlandish rite. The spectacle of two fellows eating their dinner was as mysterious and baffling today as it was yesterday, and all the days before that, but whereas Sophie would, like the rest of us, cease to seek the meaning of human gestures once she had learned to perform them, Ida would never lose her childlike vision. The world for her was a perpetual source of wonder. She had never recognised the nature of habit, the ease which it brings, and therefore it was the continuing oddity of things that fascinated her. It was not innocence, but, on the contrary, a refusal to call ordinary the complex and exquisite ciphers among which her life so tenuously hovered.

A figure approached up the road we had travelled, a tall woman in a long dress carrying a big stick. She strode along at a fast clip, swinging her arms, a mighty creature. Mario, hunched over his plate, chewed slower and slower the nearer she drew, and his eyebrows climbed up his forehead. There was indeed something exceeding strange about her. On she came, her swinging gait expressing, even at that distance, a pent-up driving irascibility. She drew level with the caravan, and flounced past, fixing us with a sullen glare. On her large head sat a frilly bonnet. Her big black boots made the stones fly. She marched past, halted, abruptly swung around, came back, and planted herself in front of us. I stared at the square blue jaw, the horny hands and thick wrists, the swollen muscles doing violence to the arms of the dress. It was a man.

'I could do with some of that grub,' he growled, and tossed the stick menacingly from one hand to the other. Mario, with his mouth full of bread, cast a cautious look up the road. Our caravan was parked on a bend, and the others were out of sight. He shrugged, and nodded to Ida, who rose and gathered together what was left of the food, two cold spuds and a lump of bread. The fellow in the dress dropped his stick and snatched the plate out of her hands and, folding his legs like a pair of scissors, plopped down in the middle of the road and began to stuff the food into his mouth, watching us the while from under his black brows. Sophie chortled, and pointed her little fat finger at him. His jaws stopped working and he scowled, and slowly began to chew again as Ida silenced the baba. He swallowed the last potato whole and threw the tin plate aside, heaved a sigh, and suddenly with an angry grunt snatched the bonnet off his head.

'Fucking yoke,' he muttered, glaring at it with great disgust.

Now, behind him, two new figures appeared on the road, one short and fat, the other tall and thin, comical fellows in blue, jogging toward us. Mario laughed.

'Eh, signora, look whosa coming.'

Our guest peered wildly over his shoulder, swore, and leapt to his feet and pounded off around the bend at high speed. The two policemen arrived, panting and heaving. They stopped, whipped off their helmets, mopped their brows, hauled up their sagging belts. Sophie chuckled again, delighted with them. The fat one jammed his helmet back on his head and pointed a threatening finger at us.

'Youse crowd,' he announced, 'are just looking to be lifted.' The finger turned and pointed up the road. 'That lad is after splitting open a man's skull. Just asking for it, youse are, and I'm the man to do it. You can tell them Sergeant Trouncer said so.'

The other one, a consumptive hulk with a sheep's long grey face, who had hovered by his superior's shoulder nodding vigorous support, now said,

'That's right, tell them that.'

We said nothing. Our apathy in the face of their threats disconcerted him. He thought for a bit.

'Just asking to be—'

'Come on, Jem, for Jesus' sake,' Trouncer roared. They galloped away. Mario laughed again, and sprang nimbly up on the ditch to watch the chase, and Ida leaned across to me with her eyes wide and her lip trembling and whispered, as though she had uncovered some enormous secret,

'Gabriel, it was a...a *man*!'

THE EXOTIC, once experienced, becomes commonplace, that is a great drawback of this world. One touches the gold and it turns to dross. It was not so with Prospero's band. I travelled with them for a year, borne onward always amid an always new and splendid oddness which sprang not merely from the excitement of new sights and sites, a new sea of faces every night, but was the essence of these fickle things joined with something more, a sense of strange and infinite possibilities: There was something always ahead of us, a nameless promise never reached and yet always within reaching distance. Perhaps because of this, the fixing of my gaze on a luminous and mythical horizon, I remember best not the circus proper, its halts and performances, but the travelling, the grate of wheels on stony roads, the thick scent of the horses, the voices floating back from the forward caravans, and the land, revolving in great slow circles around our slowly moving centre, the sad land, the lovely land.

Later in the day that we left the town, as we headed toward the distant mountains, evening sunlight broke through the clouds, and Mario, suddenly gay, began to sing. Shadows crept across the sparkling meadows. Rain fell briefly. *O mi amore, mi amore.* The road sailed down a hill toward tall sand dunes. The sun disappeared, the light around us turned a misty blue. A sulphurous glow rose and trembled above the dunes. The wind sang in the tall reeds, the unseen sea muttered. We struck away inland again, climbing now, and when I looked back I saw, in the fast-failing light, a boat with a black mast, bearing no sign of life, glide out in silence from behind a headland, a mysterious silent ship. Hill fog settled on the thorns. Night fell.

We went up into the foothills under a huge sky of stars. Black dark it was, moonless and still. Moths reeled in the glow of our lanterns. In a valley away to our left a cluster of lights bespoke a village, but the winding road we wearily followed refused to lead us there. The horses, heads bent, half asleep, traipsed on, locked in their stride. No one called a halt. A strange torpor descended on us. The air up here was thin. I sat beside Mario on the driving seat, swaying with the sway of the caravan, heedless and at peace. Vague music reached my ears. At first it seemed to come from everywhere at once, this tiny song, as though the little lights and vivid stars, the far small noises, as though the night itself were singing, but then ahead I saw at the side of the road the glow of lamplight on the undersides of leaves, and I identified the wail of pipes, the skirl of a bodhran, and Mario sprang awake and swore as the caravan ahead of us halted abruptly. A pub!

We gathered on the road. Silas stamped his feet and vigorously rubbed his backside, and the golden children yawned. Sybil, rocking Sophie in her arms, muttered under her breath. The pub was a low dingy place with a thatched roof. There was a brown opaque window dimly lit, a lantern hanging beside a crooked door, and a suggestion of turf smoke up in the darkness. Tall poplars glimmered. The wild music issued forth along with a gush of porter fumes through an open vent above the door. Silas entered, and the uproar inside ceased immediately. We shuffled in behind him, pushing and shoving sleepily. He stuck his hands into his pockets and considered the upturned faces of old men and boys, flushed youths, wild-eyed women. He grinned.

'Good evening, friends.'

None replied, but at the back someone laughed, a glass chimed, and the piper, a cadaverous fellow with a shock of lank black hair hanging over one eye, struck up another tune, the bodhran joined in with its truculent booming, and the conversation started up again. We made our way to the bar. The publican was a tubby little man with a red nose and a long apron.

'Grand evening.'

'Indeed it is,' said Silas. 'I think, ah, a glass of porter all round, and a small one for myself, to oil the joints. And you'll have one yourself?'

'Ah no.'

'Ah do.'

'Well...'

'Your health.'

'Good luck to you, sir.'

That was my first taste of porter. Frightful stuff, I must admit, for I am no hard-drinking broth of a boy, but, taken there, that brew, black and bitter, harbinger of a wild mordant gaiety, seemed to me, and still seems, to carry the savour of the country itself, this odd little land. I stood with an elbow on the bar behind me and a heel hooked on the footrail, trying to make the glass look at home in my unpractised hand, and surveyed the room. The topers were dressed in their Sunday best. It must have been a holiday, or a holyday, perhaps some feast of the Queen of May. Much raucous laughter tumbled out of gap-toothed mouths, and the voices and the strange macaronic talk clashed in the smoky air like the sounds of battle. A fat woman with a red face was copiously weeping, rocking back and forth on a stool between two sheepish, speechless men. The cadaverous piper, hunched over his reeds, swung into a gay dance tune, but his long face registered only a deeper melancholy. There is in the happiest of that music a profound thread of grief, never broken, equivalent to but not springing from the sustained drone note, an implacable mournfulness, and so, although the jig made the glasses sing, the fat woman wept and wept, rocking her sadness to sleep, and the two old men, with their hands on their knees and their jaws munching, sat and stared, with nothing to say.

Maybe I was already drunk, no telling what a sip of porter will do to you, but one minute Silas and the rest were standing beside me, the next they were scattered about the room, joining the party. Silas was engaged in what, from the angle of his chin, appeared to be a furtive conversation with a red-haired boy or small man whose face was hidden from me. Ida had borrowed the bodhran from its master, a boy with buck teeth who hovered awkwardly behind her, shuffling his feet, his face clenched in a grin of embarrassment. Mario, on the whistle, joined the piper in his song. Magnus and Sybil, with the sleeping and swaddled Sophie wedged between them, were huddled on a crowded bench in the corner where a decrepit little old man with no teeth and extraordinary knees was dancing, capering and prancing wildly, his boots banging the flagstones. Rainbird conjured cards out of the air to the delight and fright of two wide-eyed, pretty, painfully shy little girls. The golden children were, ominously, nowhere to be seen. Only Ada, in a sulk, stayed by me, slumped against the bar.

I began to play a game, idly at first and then with some excitement. I would close my eyes and then, every few seconds or so, blink rapidly. Not much of a game ? Each time I blinked I carried back into the gloom an image of arrested movement, the old man frozen in mid-air, Silas with his arm uplifted, the fat woman with a finger stuck in her red eye, and it came to me with the clarity and beauty of a mathematical statement that all movement is composed of an infinity of minute stillnesses, not one of which is exactly the same as any other and yet not so different either. It was enormously pleasing, this discovery of fixity within continuity. I elbowed my way outside, and out there in the fragrant darkness and the silence, yes, it was the same, I mean the same principle of continually fluctuating stasis held good, but the shifts and stillnesses here were vast and difficult to distinguish, but I distinguished them. And I saw something else, namely that this was how I lived, glancing every now and then out of darkness and catching sly time in the act, but such glimpses were rare and brief and of hardly any consequence, for time, time would go on anyway, without *my* vigilance.

Soon my rhapsodising under the glimmering poplars was interrupted when the others came tumbling out of the pub. The children, I gathered, had been found doing something frightful in the jakes, and they and their keepers were ejected. Silas peered at me in the dark, swaying and belching.

'Come along, Caligula, come along.'

Later, lying in my bunk in the caravan, with Mario near me emitting a kind of low hum as he sorted through his file of phantasmal ladies, I thought about the pub and the people, the piper, the weeping woman, the ancient dancer, and I felt stirring deep within me a strange and unexpected emotion which as yet I could not name, which soon settled back into hiding, and then in drowsiness my thoughts wandered afar over the dark fields and lakes, the rivers, the murmuring woods. On the point of sleep my mind made a last effort to stay awake, and my foot jerked, my teeth clenched themselves, and the essence of all I had seen that day, spring rain on the road, a black ship, curlews crying, the residue of all this spun on the last remaining tip of wakefulness like one of Mario's discs on its stick, and as I sank down into the dark I carried one word with me, that word which gives me so much trouble, which is, time.

AT THE END of the spring we stopped in a little seaside village in the south. It was a pleasant enough place, sharply divided between the whitewashed hovels of the natives at one end and, at the other, handsome holiday villas perched on promontories or retiring behind cypresses, not a few of them unshuttered and loud with children even in this early part of the year. We camped in a meadow behind the beach. The weather was glorious, days full of sun and glass, soft black nights with stars. At dawn, as the mist lifted, rabbits came out of the ground and scampered heedlessly under our wheels, into Magnus's traps. We feasted on stew and new potatoes, buttermilk and brown bread. The circus drew capacity audiences. It was a good time. We should have known, with all this, that our carefree days were numbered, that our happiness was ending. For we were happy, in our way.

There were eggs too, and jugs of thick milk, purchased from a farm nearby. There I went each morning, barefoot through the dewy drenched grass, swiping at butterflies with the milkcan. The farmhouse was a crooked affair, long and low, in need of new thatch, with tiny windows and a warped green door. Violets flourished in the filth of the yard, among the cowflop. The hall was suffused with furry yellow light, tranquil and still. I stood in the silence curling my toes on the cool tiles and waited for the daughter of the house. The doorway framed a patch of yard where brilliant sunlight shone on stylised chickens, a mongrel scratching its ear, two sparrows staring at a breadcrumb. It was odd to be inside a house again, to step across a solid floor and hear no axle creak, no horse stir. Mag came down the stairs at the end of the hall, her arms lifted, hands doing something to her hair at the back.

'Uh,' she said sleepily.

She went ahead of me across the yard tugging her brown sack-like smock into something close to her own shape underneath it. Mag was a squat heavy girl, all bone and muscle, a year or two older than I, with fuzzy red hair and a button nose and hands like cut steaks. It will seem extraordinary, but when I saw her the first time my heart skipped a beat, that hair, those odd blue eyes, although how I could picture her, even for a moment, in a white dress under a lilac tree I cannot say. Still, I was no great judge of female beauty, and I imagine that Mag appeared to me as pretty as any other. I was at that time an innocent lad to whom the dark damp side of life was still another country. I began my journey a virgin, and ended it still unsullied, but I am not ignorant of certain facts, and if here they create a somewhat twisted view of the basic acrobatic duet I insist that the warp is in the facts and not my recounting of them.

The hens lived in a wire run behind the cowshed. Mag knelt in the soiled straw and reached inside the little hut where the nests were. How odd the eggs seemed with their smooth self-sufficiency and perfect form among the crooked posts and torn wire, straw, shit, Mag's big red hands. She lifted them into the brown paper-bag with care, almost with reverence, while those ludicrous birds pranced around us, outraged and quivering. As the bag filled she reached deeper into the hut, and then paused and frowned and slowly withdrew her arm. She opened her fist between us, and there on her palm a tiny yellow chick waggled its stumpy wings and emitted a feeble cheep. We stared at the little creature, astonished that life could exist in that minuscule form, and suddenly Mag thrust it back into the hut and we fled, disturbed and obscurely embarrassed.

We went into the dairy, a long stone room with white walls and a whiter ceiling. The vacant milking stalls were whitewashed, the bare floor scrubbed. The light through the little windows was limpid and delicate. In here a silence reigned such as I have never experienced anywhere else, something like that frail nothingness which persists long after a churchbell has dropped its last chime into the pale upper airs of morning. Mag took the lid from the churn and ladled milk into my can, great dollops of it, filling the white room with a white fragrance. She seemed preoccupied and feverish. She splashed milk on her black laceless boots and gave a brief frantic squeal of laughter.

It seems incredible that we did not speak during all that followed, but I can remember no words, only glances and advances, sudden retreats like complex dance steps, and, perhaps in place of words, small modulations, readjustments in the silence between us. Mag offered me the can. I tried to take it. She would not let go. I stepped back. She put the can down on the floor. I cleared my throat. She made a determined advance, and I dived aside very neatly and fussed with the bag of eggs, placing it carefully on the floor beside the can so that nothing should break, terrible if an egg should break, smashed yolk on the stone, that yellow ooze! She reached a hand toward my trousers. I was terrified.

She lay down on her back in one of the milking stalls and I knelt before her, red-faced, with pains in my knees, grinning foolishly, with that lugubrious puce stalk, my faintly pulsating blunt sword of honour, sticking out of my trousers. Mag yanked her smock up over her enormous bubs and clawed at me, trying to pull me down on top of her. I stared at her shaggy black bush and would not, could not move. The situation was wholly farcical. She moaned beseechingly and lay down on her back again, turned up her eyes until only the whites were visible, and opened wide her mottled legs, and it was as though she had split open, had come asunder under my eyes. I knelt and goggled at the frightful wound, horrified, while my banner drooped its livid head and Mag groaned and writhed. My hand shook as I reached it forward between her gaping knees and, with my eyes closed, put my finger into her. She gasped and giggled, gasped again and thrashed her arms wildly. I opened my eyes and looked at my hand. Part of me had entered another world. The notion left me breathless. How soft and silky she was in there, how immaculate. She took my hand in hers and slowly pushed my finger out and in again, out and in, smiling to herself a strange and secret smile, and all at once I was filled with compassion. This was her mortal treasure which I touched, her sad secret, and I could only pity her, and myself also, poor frail forked creatures that we were. She sat up at last, and I leaned forward to kiss her, to plant my tenderness on her cheek. She reared away from me, gave a snort of contempt at my mawkishness, and rose and fled across the yard.

I stood in the doorway and wondered if she would return. She did not. Out in the field the caravans were ranged in a circle on the rolling green, tiny at that distance, toylike, gay. The wind blew. The smell of the sea mingled oddly here with the heavy fragrance of milk. Two of the eggs were smashed. I gathered up those that remained. The cream was rising already in the can. I went out into the yard. Violets and cowshit, my life has been ever thus.

I HAVE GIVEN the impression perhaps that wherever we stopped we were greeted with a rousing cheer of welcome, or at the very worst indifference. It was not always like that. Sometimes indifference turned into a sullen resentment which seemed to spring paradoxically from part envy, part moral disapproval. That phenomenon necessitated a rapid departure, so rapid indeed that our goings then looked like high farce. A fast getaway was imperative too when our audiences went to the other extreme and worked themselves into such a paroxysm of excitement that we were all, performers, props, stage, everything, in danger of being trampled by stampeding boots and horny bare feet. In Wexford once a full house displayed its appreciation so strenuously that it brought the house down, the tent collapsed, and in the mêlée that followed two tiny tots and an octogenarian were smothered. You could not have seen our heels for the dust.

Official disapproval was worse. Some rat-faced fellow would arrive with a writ just as the last patrons had paid their pennies and the performance was about to begin, and then, feeling foolish in our makeup and our costumes, we would shuffle our feet outside the tent while Silas in the middle of the field vainly argued our case, acting out in dumb show before the queen's man our mute bafflement and resentment. I think it was better, I mean less dispiriting, when they swept aside the formalities and sent against us a squad of soldiers tramping behind a mounted officer, who placed an elegant hand on his knee and, leaning discreetly down, quietly ordered us to move. There was no arguing with those gleaming bared bayonets. I am thinking now of the last time they put the skids under us, the last time before the country became engrossed with disaster and no one bothered about us anymore.

It was a bright day in early summer, I remember it. We were campèd on a hill above a little town with a bridge and a glittering river, narrow streets, a steeple. The first performance the night before had been well received, and we rose in the morning with that calm elation which always followed a successful première. Magnus caught a couple of rabbits, and I was sent with them to Angel. I found her in the big caravan, standing by the table with her sleeves rolled up, slicing a lump of turnip. Silas was there too, collar and braces undone, bearded in lather, shaving himself before a bit of cracked mirror. He lifted the razor in a greeting.

'Gabriel, my boy, good morrow.'

Angel took the still warm furry dead brutes and slit their bellies. The vivid entrails spilled across the table, magenta and purple polyps, tender pink cords, bright knots of blood, giving off a nutty brown odour. She hacked off the paws, chopping through bone, lopped off the head, peeled the skin. Into the big black pot it went, that painfully nude flesh, the turnip too, sliced carrots, parsnip, thyme and other aromatic things. Silas, beating the strop with the razor, lifted his head and sniffed, the wings of his red nose fluttering delicately.

'Ah,' he sighed fervently, 'ahh, grub.'

Angel said nothing. Her hair was tied back in a greasy pigtail. An odd woman, our Angel. She rarely spoke, rarely even looked directly at anyone, but seemed always preoccupied by some abiding and malicious joke. If she did look at one it was with a brief but intense and probing stare, one eyebrow lifted, lips compressed. When she spoke, her words were scarred by elisions, run together into one sound like a bark, the tone jangling with derision and black amusement. Sometimes she would laugh without apparent cause, a rumbling hiccupping noise like that of something soft and heavy rolling about in a barrel. In spite of her seeming intangibility she presided over all the doings of the circus with a mysterious strength, her massive trunk, with that flat yellowish face set on the front of it, planted among us like an implacable and ribald totem. I found her unsettling and kept out of her way when I could, for she seemed to me to personify, more than any of the others, the capriciousness, mockery and faint menace on which the circus was founded. She wiped her bloodied hands on a rag.

'Food, food,' said Silas, towelling his face with such vigour that it gleamed. 'Dear me, how I miss the splendours of my better days!' He came and sat down by the table with a comically mournful look. 'I remember a feast which my good friend Trimalchio once laid on for me. Such delicacies! Listen. Around the fountain, with the soothing sound of water in our ears, we ate olives, dormice smothered in honey and poppyseed, dishes of fragrant little sausages. Inside, where a hundred perfumed candles burned, we reclined on silken couches set so that we could look down over the twilit city, the hills. There we had goblets of sea-red wine with orioles baked in pastry. Next, the gleaming Nubians carried to us trays of capon and sowbelly, a hare with wings like a tiny Pegasus. The gravy boats...well well, forget the gravy boats. Then came a huge wild sow, a daunting brute, whose flank, split open, released a cloud of live thrushes. This pig was not to eat, only for show, for next there came a gargantuan hog which had for guts great rings of sausages and spiced blood puddings. There were fresh fruits and sweetmeats, eggs, pastry thrushes filled with raisins and nuts and sugar. There were quinces and pears and blushing peaches. At last came a platter of roast pork, pork roasted and boned and shaped into the form of fish and birds that swam in a gravy pond on which, ah my friends!, a goose fashioned from pork swam proudly. Great Jove, what a feed. And now? To what am I reduced?' He puckered his mouth in distaste. '*Rabbit stew!*'

Angel paid no attention to him. She counted off on her fingers silently the ingredients in the pot, paused a moment, pondering, and suddenly gave one of her frightful guffaws.

'No spuds,' she said, greatly tickled. 'No spuds!'

Feet beat on the steps of the caravan and the twins tumbled in, struggling and giggling, fighting each other through the narrow doorway.

'Theserverishere, theserverishere,' they chanted, 'theserverisherewiththepaper!'

Silas jumped up and swiped at them with the towel. They fled amid screams of laughter.

'Young ruffians,' he said, shaking his head, and then stopped and stared with slowly dawning horror at his reflection in the cracked mirror. 'What did they...? The *server*!'

He whirled about and kicked shut the lower half of the door. The process-server, hopping up the steps, was rapped smartly on the knees. He was a weedy fellow in a green jacket, black britches and a preposterous battered high hat. His long thin nose was raw and red, his pale eyes were moist. He brandished the writ at Silas, who stood inside the halfdoor with his hands clasped behind his back.

'Are you— ?' the server began.

'I am not,' Silas said, and grinned.

'I'm serving this writ on you in the name of—'

'You are not.'

Now it was the server's turn to be amused. His pinched face twitched with a sly little smirk.

'O I see,' said he. 'It's like that, is it ? Well let me tell you, we've had your kind before. Would you rather have the squaddies ? They're clumsy lads, they are. Things get broke when they arrive. Heads and things.'

'Are you threatening me ?'

'I am, aye.'

'Uncouth fellow!' Silas roared, and slammed the top half of the door. There was a cry of pain outside, and the sound of feet clattering down the steps. Silas waited a moment, took a deep breath, hitched up his braces and flung open the door again. The server with streaming eyes stood below the steps gingerly fingering his bleeding nose. Silas charged at him, but veered abruptly and scampered away around the side of the caravan. The server stumbled after him with one hand clamped on his hat, the other feebly waving the writ. I poked my head out the door in time to see Silas come pounding around from the left. The server doubled back, they met, and Silas skidded to a halt with a scream of mock terror. Soon they were running in circles around the field, the server wiping his eyes as he ran, Silas puffing and laughing and flapping his arms. The twins, over by the tent, danced up and down and cheered gleefully. Others came out to watch, Magnus and Sybil, Ida wringing her hands, Mario scowling. Silas and his pursuer, exhausted, abandoned the race at last. Silas jammed his hands into his pockets.

'I don't want it,' he cried. 'I don't *want* that thing.'

'It's not a question of wanting!'

'Listen, my man—'

130

'*Will you take it!*'

'But please—'

'Right! This is one for Captain Tuzo to settle. We'll see how you get on with him and his men. I'll have the lot of you threw out of here before the day is done.'

'Listen, my dear Malvolio, be reasonable—'

'O that'll be all right now,' said the server, with an assumed calmness, lifting a hand to straighten his hat. 'That'll be all right.' He stuffed the writ into his pocket, put a finger to the side of his swollen nose and deposited at Silas's feet a gout of blood and snot. 'Now!' he said, and left.

He was as good as his word, for within the hour Rainbird, who had been sent to scout, came back pedalling furiously with the news that the troops were on their way. We hauled down the tent, hitched up the horses, fled. Angel's stew was overturned and lost in the confusion. The army, at a distance, saw us go, lost interest in us and turned back to the town. Out on the roads the air was vile with a smell of rot, and in the ruined fields people stood motionless in groups, baffled and silent. The potato crop had failed.

I WAS NOW midway upon my journey, stumbling in darkness, and the day came when I could no longer ignore the fact that the darkness was of my own making. Accordingly, I began to consider seriously my past and my future. It was the present I should have thought about, but the present is unthinkable. It did colour my thoughts, however, with of all things a certain insouciance. The imminence of disaster brings not piety and a concern for last things, it brings frivolity and laughter. I think that we shall all be drunk and gay, dancing a jig in the nude, when the apocalypse arrives to annihilate us at last. Famine hung above us like black smoke, and under that black cloud I wondered, with incredible levity, if it might not be better for me to cast aside the notion of a quest.

The story of my sister, the stolen child, had been laughed at. That laughter woke me from a dream. No, not a dream precisely, but a waking, necessary fantasy. Necessary, yes. If I had not a solid reason to be here, travelling the roads with this preposterous band, then my world threatened to collapse, for I still believed then that life was at least reasonable. The future must have a locus! If not, what was the point? It was a cold bleak sea in which to be adrift. Still, for all the dangers it entailed, I admitted at last that the search for this doubtful sister could no longer sustain me. Well then, if she did not exist—and I could not admit *that* much— how explain the hints and discrepancies in my past, the tiny corners of enormous secrets revealed, and that one bold forthright message delivered to me the night before I left? I went over these fragments again and again, and always there was distilled out of

all my considerations one thrilling and inexplicable name—
Prospero. Only the name emerged, no reasons, explanations,
revelations, except for a barely substantial sense of a connection
somewhere between a red-haired boy and a story told of the
shadowy master of revels himself. I wearied my brain with wondering and then stumbled in a kind of trance to see Rainbird, but
when I saw him I had nothing to say, for it was not Rainbird
himself I had sought but something for which he was a paltry
symbol. I turned away, angry and frustrated, and the dwarf
smirked and said,

'Find her yet?'

If she did exist, this sister whom I called Rose, I did not know
why, what chance had I of finding her? The world is full of
people, and how many of them know from where they come?
A crack opens, a creature falls in, the crack closes. We were half a
day's journey out of the town when Mario beside me suddenly
cried,

'Sophie! Where is she? You seen her, eh?'

I had not seen her. He leaped down and ran ahead to the forward caravans. Soon he returned, pale and frantic.

'She'sa gone! My baba! We *lost* her.'

There was a touch of astonishment mixed with his grief. He
trotted beside me for a while, wringing his hands and muttering,
then he fell behind and stopped and looked helplessly this way
and that, turned and sped off down the road we had travelled.
We halted and called after him, but he would not hear. He did
not return that night. The choice was clear before us, we must
either return and face the soldiers or move on and leave him and
the baby to their fate. Silas paced up and down in the black caravan
after supper while the rest of us sat in silence watching him. He
avoided our eyes for as long as he could and at last turned to us
and threw out his arms.

'What can we do?' he wailed. 'We can't go back!' He lumbered
to his knees before Ada and took her hands in his. 'What shall we
do, my dear? It's your child, you...' He searched desperately for
a description of Mario. 'Your friend,' he said faintly.

Ada shrugged.

'We can't go back.' She glanced at the rest of us. 'Can we?'

No, there was no going back. We used the soldiers as a name
for our fear, but it was the murrain stalking our heels that drove

us on. We travelled high into the mountains, thinking surely, up there, away from the towns, there would be no shortage of food. We were wrong. At first the full significance of the potato failure did not strike us. There would be a famine, that much we knew, and a few people might starve, but not us. The spud had never been our staple diet, and was there not a spectrum of other vegetables, of meat and bread, of milk, eggs? There was not, after a little while. As news of the blight spread, only marginally swifter than the blight itself, the fields were stripped, and what was left, the great meadows of corn, the cattle, these were reserved for export to another land, and trade would not be disrupted or even interrupted because of a mere famine. The first deaths were reported as the grainships sailed.

Up in the mountains we did not starve, but hunger was a constant baleful companion, as yet only a vague gnawing in the pits of our stomachs, but what horrors it promised! O I do not say that we were desperate up there. Like the rest of the country, things would have to get much worse before we would admit our plight. There was still the occasional rabbit, a loaf of bread. We developed a taste for nettle soup. It was summer, after all, glorious weather. Angel made sloe wine, and one night we got wildly drunk, every one, even the children, but in the morning with the hangovers the lethargy came back, that strange abiding paralysis which had attacked the spirit of the circus. In every village where we stopped Silas looked at the tumbledown hovels, the shuttered pubs, the drawn grey faces and remote eyes staring blankly, and shook his head, saying no, this was no place for our talents. At last we even stopped travelling. There seemed no point to it anymore. The summer sunshine took on a muddy cast, became somehow dimmed, as though our eyes were filled with water.

But what a spot it was where we chose to stop, a little green cleft between two hills with a stream and an oak tree and a view down a long verdant valley where the shadows of clouds swam down the mountain slopes all day, and larks at noon set the sky quivering with their music. It was here, one morning in July, that Mario caught up with us. I watched him make his way across the valley, plodding slowly along on a stick with his head bent. He looked like an old man. His clothes were in tatters. The soldiers had beaten him. His eyes were strange. He sat wrapped in silence among us for a long time and then stirred and sighed.

'Nothing,' he said. 'Gone.'

One of his hands lay before him on the table like a dead white animal.

MY WANING FAITH in the existence of my sister was revived briefly and unexpectedly by Sybil. Now for Sybil there were only two kinds of people, those who came under Silas's sphere of influence, and those other altogether splendid creatures who came under hers. I do not know on what evidence she decided who was whose, but in her eyes the distinction was very clear, and those who could not be considered by any stretch of the imagination to belong to either camp she ignored so totally that they might have been transparent. Angel, being neutral, she would not see, but toward Mario, one of Silas's men, she bore an enmity so unrelenting, even after the loss of his daughter had broken him, that one was forced to admire it. Of course, when I say Silas's influence I mean that he was merely a handy yardstick by which she measured the depraved and raucous, vulgar side of life, that life lived in the nasty world of *the people* which horrified her so, and which, she firmly believed, touched at no point her private planet of rose petals. She saw herself as a delicate bloom struggling for survival on a dung heap, and the shrewishness, the foul temper, the coldness, these she regarded as but the traits of an aristocratic nature. Such was Sybil. Well well, blind pride is no crime, whatever they may say, and I think I must have loved her a little in my odd way if this feeling now, in deceptive September, can be trusted. She looked on me as Silas's pet prodigy and treated me accordingly, which is why I was surprised and frightened when she showed me what for her can only be called tenderness.

It rained all that day, drops like fat pearls fell out of a bright sky and turned our spot into a spongy green quagmire. Birds sat in silence despondently in the bushes shaking the wet out of their plumage, and the rocks dripped and streamed. It was one of those days when time seems to have paused out of a lack of interest. I was passing by Silas's caravan when I heard my name called softly through the open doorway. Inside, when I could see through the gloom, I found Sybil alone on a bench under the little window sitting with her legs crossed, one foot idly swinging, the fingers of her right hand resting against her cheek. She wore a long black skirt, a white blouse and narrow patent leather boots. I realised anew what an exquisite creature she was, with that vivid red hair, the sculptured face, pale slender hands, but now I saw also how much she had changed in the last weeks. Something had happened to her face, a minute but devastating change. Her left eye seemed to droop a fraction lower than the right, and this imbalance gave to what had been her cool measured gaze a querulous, faintly crazed cast. Her cheeks too had sunk, and their former bloom had now become a silvery sheen. Her fits of fury were more frequent, less comprehensible. She lacerated Silas for no reason that could be discerned other than his existence. Her rages fell asunder in the middle, the words dried up and she was left trembling, leaning out to one side, hiccupping speechlessly, her hands clenched and a red stain spreading slowly across her forehead. Then she would stumble away with her head bent, hands over her face, and, after an awkward silence, someone, usually Magnus, would rise and follow her with heavy tread while the rest of us sat and waited with bated breath for the first long piercing wail. Now she lifted her face to the pearly light in the window and gazed out across the valley.

'Is it true you're searching for your sister? They say you are. That's very...romantic.'

She spoke quietly and gravely. I could think of nothing to say, and I suppose, being young, I squirmed, pursed my lips, sighed. She looked at me with her crooked icy blue eyes.

'What is her name?'

'Rose. I—I think.'

'Rose. Ah. And you know what she looks like? You have a picture?'

'Yes.'

She smiled. I would have preferred her cold stare. Her foot swung faster. She twined a lock of hair around her fingers.

'I might be able to help you,' she said. 'Would you like me to help you, Gabriel? There are a lot of things here that you don't know about. Silas tells me things. He has a plan, you know. Soon, soon we'll be leaving here, and then I could help you, if you...' She paused and frowned, as though searching for something that I might have to offer. 'If you were to become my... friend. That's all I have ever asked of anyone, that they be friends with me. They say I'm a bitch, O yes they do, Gabriel, they say that, but it's not true, not true at all. I am only...unhappy.'

The voice caressed me, it was almost a physical sensation, the warm words touching my eyelids, my hot cheeks. If I gave her any answer it must have been a tiny whine. She offered me her hand but I would not take it.

'Gabriel? Don't you like me either?' Her eyes narrowed, and although she did not seem to move her lips I could see now the glint of her sharp white teeth. The hand she offered began to tremble, and the fingers danced like pale snakes. 'Why don't you like me. Gabriel!' She stood up, and a handkerchief fell from her sleeve and fluttered to the floor. 'Little beast,' she snarled. 'You're like the rest, you hate me. Well we'll see, my man, we'll see who needs who, yes, yes. I could save you but I won't, not after this. I'll laugh, yes I'll laugh, when they string you up and gut you. Now *get out!*'

I turned to go, relieved and terrified all at once, but before I could take a step she swept past me through the door and plunged down the steps into the rain. I picked up her handkerchief, gingerly, gingerly, and put it on the bench. There was a flurry behind me and she was back again, staring at me wildly. Her hair was laced with shining raindrops. She fell to her knees and threw her arms around my hips, and with her head against my stomach she wept, such bitter tears, such black sorrow.

'I'm so unhappy,' she sobbed, 'so unhappy!'

I wanted to laugh, although there was nothing funny, nothing at all, and now I am surprised to find that I still want to laugh, thinking of that scene, and still I can see nothing in it that merits laughter. Strange. What brought forth that grief? I hesitate, I am unwilling, I hardly dare to voice the notion which, if it did not come to me then comes to me now, the insane notion that perhaps it was on her, on Sybil, our bright bitch, that the sorrow of the country, of those baffled people in the rotting fields, of the stricken eyes staring out of hovels, was visited against her will and even without her knowledge so that tears might be shed, and the inexpressible expressed. Does that seem a ridiculous suggestion? But I do not suggest, I only wonder.

THAT SUMMER ENDED. We were relieved, I think. September suited better our sombre mood. Every autumn seems like the last. Not that the weather turned. The sun still shone, mocking us with its gaiety, and the little stream still chattered, but on the hills the trees were dusted with copper, autumn gold was in the air, and a smell of smoke at evening. But all that time, gone! Our lethargy frightened us. There were other, worse things. Terrible rumours were brought back from the lowland with each week's dwindling stock of provisions. The people had no food down there, they were eating grass, the bark of trees, dried leaves. Children were seen gobbling fistfuls of clay. Bands of savage-fanged hermaphrodites stalked the countryside at night killing and looting. Some said they ate their victims. These preposterous stories made us laugh yet filled us with a quiet terror which we could not admit to ourselves or to each other. The admission would have made it worse, and so we played with exaggeration as a means of keeping reality at bay. It did not work. Reality was hunger, and there was no gainsaying that.

We did find a way to neutralise the truth if not quite banish it, and that was by inventing taller stories than the tallest the lowland could produce. One day, however, the trick backfired in our faces when Silas told us of the ingenious and economical method which he swore they used to bury their dead down there. So many were dying, all of them penniless, that a full-scale funeral with all the trimmings was impossible for each of them, until someone invented the false coffin. This was a splendid affair, craftsman-built from the best wood, with brass handles and gleaming bolts, paid for out of a general fund.

'Expensive, that's true,' said Silas, 'but here's the beauty of it, listen. A large town would need no more than two of them, say three at the most. Why? Well, the stiff is popped in, see, bolted down, out to the graveyard, hold the contraption over the hole, the druid says the prayers, then someone presses a switch and plop! down goes your man, fill up the grave, shut the trapdoor and you're ready for the next cadaver! How about that now for a notion?'

We laughed into our fists and stamped our feet, held our sides, the story was so droll, so ludicrous. An hour later Mario and Magnus returned from a vain search for food down below, and when they told us of a funeral they had witnessed, Silas's story was no longer fantasy, although the coffin they had seen had been no splendid casket but a plain wood box with an ill-fitting panel underneath which was wrenched out to release the body. Magnus remembered the dull thump inside the grave.

Now we ate only what the countryside could give us, wild berries, crab apples stewed, an occasional rabbit or a hare, some roots even. Once we ate a fox which Magnus had inadvertently trapped. Such a beautiful creature, we wept as we ate, for the fox and for ourselves, but beauty had no place in that world, the times were such that there was nothing to do with beauty but destroy it. Ah Ida, my gentle Ida. I went with her one afternoon to gather blackberries. It was a perfect autumn day, full of light and woody smells, glittering and crisp. We wandered far away from the camp, across the hill and down into another valley where the bushes were heavy with fruit. Ida sang as we picked. We ate our fill of the tender berries. They tasted of summer and sunshine. Disaster waits for moments like this, biding its time.

'Gabriel,' she said, 'have you really got a sister?'

'Yes I have. Of course I have.'

She watched me with that odd awed gaze of hers, dropping her pickings absentmindedly into the grass beside the can.

'But how will you *find* her?' she cried very softly, and leaned toward me, full of concern. I shrugged, and looked away across the mountains with a frown. When I turned to her again there were tears in her eyes.

'Poor Mario,' she said.

She wandered away then across the meadow, and I lay down in the warm grass behind the bushes. I was half asleep when I heard them, and scrambled to my knees and peered out over the briars. On the far side of the valley three soldiers were making their way laboriously down the hillside. Great hulking fellows they were, drunk I think, staggering and stumbling on the stony ground, clutching at each other, their rifles joggling on their backs. Once down in the valley they halted suddenly and stood with their heads lifted, listening. On a breeze there came to me faintly the sound, which they had heard, of Ida's piping song. They crept into the bushes and soon the singing stopped and there was a scream, a scream such as I have never heard again, and I have heard many, expressing as it did so little fear, but a terrible depth of desolation and woe. I raced across the valley, into the bushes, heedless of the thorns tearing my legs, but I could not find them, and there were no more cries to guide me.

I searched for hours, pacing the hills in a numbed trance. Rain fell. As the light began to fail I found them on the road. Only one soldier remained. He staggered ahead of me dragging Ida along by one limp arm. She was a heavy load, lying down on her back like that and her heels bouncing over the stones. He stopped and swore and began to beat her with the butt of his rifle, smacking her skull in a bored weary tattoo and saying over and over in a reedy voice, *You nowghty girl you! You nowghty girl you!* Poor Ida lay there silently, her head rolling from side to side under the blows as the rain fell on her. The soldier looked at me and paused with the rifle lifted above his shoulder. He looked at me, and at Ida, at me again, with his mouth hanging open, and then shrugged and lowered the rifle.

'Fucking micks,' he muttered. 'Barmy!'

He reeled away down the road. I carried Ida on my shoulders back to the camp. How did I carry that weight so far? Perhaps it was not far. Silas said nothing. After all, he had been expecting this or something like it, some disaster, he was not surprised. Her blood was all over me, even in my hair. We wrapped her in a blanket and laid her on her bunk. In the night she woke and cried out for Mario. I found him lying in our caravan staring at the flame of a guttering candle. I told him he was needed for a deathbed scene. He looked up at me expressionlessly for a long time with those strange still eyes.

'Fuck off,' he said softly at last, and turned his face to the wall. It made no difference. She was already dead. I arrived back as Silas was closing her eyes, and it was as if he had closed a door on a whole world.

ODD, BUT I can remember no tears. Lamentations seemed somehow superfluous. If one stopped and thought for a moment about her death one said *yes, really, it's logical enough,* and it was, with the grotesque logic of the times. When we looked back now we saw that it was for this death we had waited, suspended up here in the mountains, as though a sacrifice were necessary before we could move on, and the sacrifice of course was the slaughter of innocence. Or is all that too subtle, too neat? We buried her next morning, wrapped in a white shroud, beside the stream, and there was silence but for the noise of the spade and the larks singing, no prayers, no eulogies, nothing.

With the murder of the innocent went our innocence, and in its place came something brutal and icecold. We struck camp that very day and travelled down into the plain. It was strange to be on the move again, to hear the wheels groan and the hoofs stamping. We had thought to leave death behind us in the mountains, but down here it was everywhere in the air. It was as bad as we had been told, worse. There was a smell of death. No beasts grazed in the meadows, no smoke rose from chimneys. Children sat motionless at the crossroads staring out of huge round eyes. We passed by a woman lying laughing in a ditch. The fields lay fallow. After a week we reached the coast and headed southwards in a storm. The wind roared for days, buffeting the frail walls of the caravans, filling our mouths and eyes with salt. When the wind dropped it was winter, and there was ice in the hedgerows, the fallen leaves were brittle with frost, and the air grew fangs. Now the hoofs on the road had a steely ring, and the mornings

143

were black as pitch. My teeth went bad. We had no money, no food. That was a terrible time.

We came to a town, and an echo rose out of my past. Yes, there was the broken rampart, the belltower, the barracks. I was, if you like, home. There was no welcome there for me. Everything was the same and yet changed. Silas saw me looking, and smiled.

'Aye, Master Little Boots, you recognise this place? Here we end our journey.' He winked. '*I know someone...*'

We rumbled down the empty main street. A bell chimed thrice, three sombre strokes. Children threw stones at us in an eerie, malevolent silence, and fled. We entered an empty crooked square. Here the houses along two sides were fine bright edifices, wine-red brick and white windows curtained with lace, while their counterparts facing them were low thatched shanties, ruined, most of them, with their walls breached as though by cannonshot. The roofs were in tatters. Shattered fireplaces hung in mid-air. Even the worst of these wrecks were inhabited. One, its front wall gone completely, was like a grotesque cutaway illustration of the times. On the lower floors an emaciated mother was cooking something frightful in a black pot while her brood of rickety children scuttled around her, and upstairs the father, tended by a dutiful daughter, lay on a pallet made of sacking, doing his best to die. They paid us not the slightest heed as our gaping cavalcade went past.

At one of the two streets leading out of the square Silas called a halt. We reined in the horses and waited, for what, we did not know, looking expectantly toward Silas, who sat in his doorway, puffing on his pipe, and considered the sky above the houses with a faint dreamy smile. Down at the end of the street which his caravan blocked a sliver of sea was visible. The silence was strange, deep yet light as the chill winter air, tingling, itching to be broken, as it was at last by a thin high-pitched whistle. Silas's ears seemed to twitch, but still he gazed upward, puffing and smiling. There was a stirring in the rubble of one of the shattered houses, and a small woman in a wide flowered dress with her head hidden by a black shawl stepped out into the square, shook the dust off herself like a dog shaking water out of its fur, and hurried toward us. There was something in that walk, the way the arms sawed, haunches rolled, shoulders strained at the delicate stuff of the gown, that reminded me of another time, a road, a chase.

She reached Silas's caravan and stopped, and he, with a great show of surprise, whipped the pipe out of his mouth and bent to help her up beside him. We craned our necks and stared. What woman was this, rising out of the ground in a strange town? She put her foot on the rim of the wheel and Silas yanked her arm, the wind blew, the dress billowed, and there was revealed to us, instead of the pink knickers, say, we had expected, a pair of coarse tweed trousers hitched up around the knees and tied with binder-twine. The two, already deep in conversation, disappeared into the caravan, and we were left with the silence again. Someone laughed uneasily. I was excited and obscurely alarmed, for I had seen in that strange man-woman, behind the echo of that other one we had fed as he fled from the peelers, another fainter echo out of a deeper past. I began to step down from the seat, intending to creep up and spy on their secret conference, but Mario reached out a hand and held me fast.

'Is none your business, boy,' he growled, and it was at that moment that my real fear began. That black shawl was there to hide more than mere gender.

Half an hour passed. Magnus and Ada played a game of cards. The twins went back for another look at the starving family. Sybil sat on a wooden box behind Silas's caravan, staring intently at nothing and brushing her hair, stroke after slow stroke, endlessly. Now a noise that had begun as a vague distant buzzing became the quavering voice of a concourse lifted in song. The sound drew nearer, rising and falling like an ill heart's beat behind the houses up at the other end of the square. We turned our faces thither, awaiting the appearance of the singers, but instead there crept out of the mouth of the street a horde of squat grey creatures, scores of them, crawling on their bellies and scuttling over each other's backs, or hopping in that strange way they have, as though each hop were a pounce, stopping, rising on their haunches to sniff the air with delicate snouts, their black eyes glittering. Rats! They scattered into the broken houses, and the procession arrived and crawled painfully toward us across the square like a snake with a broken back, a wavering string of emaciated townsfolk. Their sad song rose like a moan. In the van there marched a priest with cropped red hair and cracked boots holding a rough wooden cross aloft, and out at the side, stalking the line like an outrider, was a figure in a cocked hat and gaiters, white trousers, a green jacket. Strongbow! There he was, in full regalia, as preposterously plumed and groomed as ever. I almost laughed to see him, my ridiculous friend. If I threw a stone at him would he remember that day when he chased me off the town's historic ramparts? It seemed unlikely, for he had larger issues to occupy him now than the irreverence of little boys. Behind the priest a coffin was borne along on the shoulders of four stooped men. It was a small box. They were building them smaller now. Famine shrivelled its corpses. I wondered if this were one of Silas's sliding contraptions.

Singing, weaving, staring blankly, they marched across the square. In the wake of the coffin a crazed old woman stumbled, softly wailing. I recognised her. The rest looked away from her as though embarrassed by her tears. Here was no place for such a show of grief, too many were dying, silence sufficed. Silas's caravan stood in their path. The priest halted and lowered the cross, and behind him a convulsion of halting ran back through the crowd. The song trembled uncertainly, soared on one last note and faded. Strongbow came marching up, conferred briefly with the priest, then stepped up to the caravan and rapped with his fist on the window. There was no response, and he retreated a pace in confusion, stamping his heels. One of the coffin bearers moaned very softly. Strongbow cast a sidelong glance at the other caravans and their silent attentive occupants. He was about to speak when the door above him opened and Silas stepped out on the driving board and leaned down and asked,

'Well, my good man?'

Strongbow's plume bristled.

'Get this yoke on up owwa the way there!'

'I beg your pardon?'

'Get owwa the way!'

The priest pointed a shaking finger at the silent procession at his back.

'You're blocking the street,' he roared. 'Can you not see it's a funeral, man!'

'Why, so it is,' said Silas.

'You bloody get!' Strongbow cried, and made a grab at Silas's leg and missed. With a banging of boots and a clatter of buckles two peelers came running. More old friends! Sergeant Trouncer straightened his helmet and said, 'Right! what's up here?'

The consumptive constable behind him could not speak for lack of breath, but he backed up his superior officer with a fierce look out of his sheep's eyes. They all began to shout at once. The priest waved his fists, Strongbow stamped his feet and rumbled menacingly, and Sergeant Trouncer bellowed at the constable, who drew his truncheon and made to clamber up on the caravan. Silas kicked him on the side of the head, and as he toppled backward in a swoon he brought down Trouncer with him, and Trouncer clutched at Strongbow, who fell on the priest, and the four of them collapsed in a heap, flailing and roaring, and the cross poked the priest in the eye. Silas gleefully clapped his hands on his knees, the old woman shrieked, Mario began to laugh, and then the coffin exploded. Screws flew out of their sockets like a volley of shots, the lid flew open, boards splintered, and the corpse, O! that terrible swollen thing, slid down between the shoulders of the crouching bearers and rolled across the ground shedding a foul bandage in its wake like a snail's trail. Listen, listen to me, I have seen worse, I have seen things more terrible than this. The mourners fled in all directions waving their arms and screaming, and even the four felled pillars of the community scuttled away panicstricken. Only the old woman remained. She knelt and tore her hair, and laughed hysterically with that same raucous cackle I had heard long ago among the blackcurrant bushes. I stared down at the corpse lying in its wreckage. Silas lashed his horse, and the circus thundered out of the square.

OF HIM in the dress there was no sign until, a mile outside the town, he leaped down from Silas's careering caravan and vaulted a ditch, tripped on the other side and fell flat on his face, bounced up again immediately and scampered away across the fields. Our pace slackened as the panic evaporated, and then the horses would not go on, but halted and stood with lowered heads, shuddering and coughing. I got down and walked about the road in a daze. Up on the caravan Mario shook his head and laughed softly to himself.

'*Boom*,' he murmured, over and over. '*Boom !*'

Silas with his coattails flying and his black hat askew came rushing back along the line.

'Come on, come on, keep moving, no stopping yet! Get up there, Little Boots. Mario! The soldiers are after us, get going.'

He was in fine fettle, full of excitement and glee. Mario smiled at him wildly and opened wide his eyes and said,

'Boom!'

Silas halted in his tracks and began to laugh helplessly.

'Mad,' he cried, 'stark mad! Gabriel, keep your eye on him, don't let him get behind you. Crackers!' He scampered away. 'Come on now, children, come *on*!'

We whipped up the horses and turned down a boreen into a field, forded a stream and struggled up a hill of thorns, and when we reached the road again we met Rainbird pedalling furiously past us in the opposite direction. He soon returned, pale and breathless. Sergeant Trouncer and a dozen peelers, backed up by a squad of troops, were hot on our trail. They dogged us inexorably all day, until at evening we lost them. The weather turned, and a bitter wind blew up from the east. The land was hard and bare as a bone. With the cold came hunger pains. A sulphurous glow faded slowly out of the western sky, and in a bleak twilight we stopped at a pub, the same one we had visited on my first day travelling with the circus, an age past. This time there was no music. We crowded into the doorway and stared in silence at the chairs crouching empty by the tables, the lamps smoking, glasses gleaming, at our indistinct selves rippling in the mirror, and then Silas strode to the deserted bar and rapped upon it with his knuckles, and Rainbird darted under the flap of the counter and popped up grinning on the other side.

'A ball of malt, my man,' said Silas, but his words rang dully in the eerie stillness. He glared at the empty tables, daring the ghosts to show themselves, and turned to us in the doorway. 'Come in, friends, and state your pleasure. It's on the house to-night. Come!'

We entered warily, and Rainbird busied himself with bottles. The first drink went down in an uneasy silence, but as it settled on their empty bellies a kind of delirium set in immediately, and the revels began. I would take nothing, and sat in a corner nursing my hunger. Glasses fell, and a keg burst and sprayed the mirror with froth. Someone knocked over a lamp. The blazing oil sprang across the floor with a roar. They poured porter on the flames. Mario, sitting cross-legged on a table, vomited repeatedly into his lap. Something was dying here. I watched it twitching in the drunken faces that I could no longer recognise, these impenetrable masks of grey and yellow wax. For all their laughter and their shrieks the silence was still there beneath all, the anguish and the dumb longing of those whose absence sat beside us like an implacable black bird in this house of the dead. It was not hunger that was killing us, but the famine itself. The black smoke was poisoning us. The plague was here. Silas alone seemed immune, presiding over the Tötentanz with his old wicked gaiety, leaning against the bar and jogging his glass in time to the fevered rising rhythm of the dance.

I went out into the yard behind the pub. The night was moonless, tingling with ice. The wind sang over the invisible fields. I do not know how long I stood out there, gazing into the dark. Perhaps I fell asleep on my feet. The noises came to me unnoticed at first, voices and the thud of boots, clatter of metal and wood, and an oddly familiar crackling. I started back into the pub, thought better of it, and scurried around the side of the building under the poplars. One of the caravans was on fire, and there were soldiers on the road scurrying about against the glare like tin men. Away in the dark somewhere Sergeant Trouncer was roaring commands. Silas and the others blundered out of the pub and tripped over each other, swearing and squeaking. I set off at a run toward the blazing caravan. Magnus overtook me.

'*Get back, Gabriel, get back!*'

A challenge rang out nearby and I veered away, flame spurted from the muzzle of a rifle, and over my shoulder I saw by that brief livid light Magnus halt as the back of his head exploded. He went down like a stricken spider, arms and legs spinning, and in his place there popped up before me, like a sad and lovely aunt sally, the image of him dancing in a field in April rain with mouth-organ music wreathed around him like flowers. Magnus! I found a horse unharnessed and leaped upon its sagging back and rode away across the fields.

PART III

Mercury

FOAM FROM THE HORSE'S flapping lips flew back into my face and froze on my eyelashes, my cheeks, and frost burned my eyes. A sliver of moon like an icicle swung into the sky. At a ditch old Incitatus baulked and slung me over his ears. The fall loosened every tooth in my head, and my eyeballs seemed to spin in their sockets like tops. I felt that something had come loose at the back of my brain. After that wallop my reasoning shut up shop, I ceased to think, and only a frantic and basic set of instincts kept me going. I was filled with darkness. And the cold! O bitter, bitter.

I survived that night, and many others, don't ask me how, wandering the countryside, half starved, half mad too I suspect, for how long I do not know—was it weeks, months, years? I fell in with a band of tinkers who fed and clothed me and asked no questions. One night, prey to a nameless panic, I fled the camp. The roads were choked with refugees, forlorn bands coming from nowhere and going to the same place, jettisoning in their wake a spoor of broken belongings. Their charity kept me alive. God knows what they thought I was, this crazed filthy creature perched on a starved nag. Perhaps they saw in me a celestial messenger of hope, anything is possible. I was not grateful for their kindness. I despised and loathed their misery, their helplessness. My accent impressed them. Some even called me sir. Sir! What a people!

I travelled, but I did not travel far. My journey described a wide circle the centre of which was, unknown to me, the circus, carrying me with it toward its goal by some mysterious intangible magnetism. The first faltering days of spring arrived. I remember gaping in bafflement at the green buds on a tree which had been bare when I lay down under it the night before. I could not cope with the season of resurrections. One day the horse died, buckled under me and flopped on its side on the road, coughed up unspeakable stuff, kicked, and was gone. There is a point at which one decides to surrender. Under one's dancing feet a black chasm waits always, always inviting. I had felt that darkness beneath me for so long that it had come to seem like a last refuge into which I could fly, and now as I left the dead brute there on the road and plunged into the woods I was content to think that I would never again see the light of day. But life, whatever it may be, is not simple.

In a clearing deep in the wood there was a ruined cottage, rubble and weeds and a rusty bedstead, and one upright wall with a cracked mirror suspended half way up it and a shaky lean-to made of branches and bits of sacking clinging to it like a faltering parasite. Amidst the weeds a fire burned under a blackened battered can slung on a forked stick, and it was over this steaming can and its intoxicating, barely familiar smell that I was bending when a pair of fierce eyes sprang at me from the dark den under the sacking.

'Get your snout out of that!'

He sat on a stone in there with his hands clamped on his knees and glared at me, a huge fellow in a tattered overcoat and a lidless high hat. Two filthy toes stuck out of his boots, and a fearful set of yellow teeth were clenched in a hole in his beard. He spat into the fire and snarled. I thought of running away, but I knew that my legs would not work.

'Who the fuck are you?' he asked.

'Johann Livelb, sir.'

'That's a queer class of a name. Joe what?'

'Johann, sir. Livelb.'

Suddenly he cackled.

'Begod that's a mouthful all right. Sit down.'

I crept into the hovel and squatted on the ground beside him. He looked at me silently for a moment, grinding his teeth, and then turned his eyes to the fire.

'I think I'm dying, sir,' I said.

He nodded absently, and picked out a piece of stick from the bundle between his feet and threw it on the fire. Flames leaped up, and the stuff in the can bubbled fiercely. My stomach heaved.

'Bit of grub, there,' he observed, and looked down at me and winked. 'Meat. Can't remember when I had it last. The country's in an awful fucking state. They're dropping like flies. Never seen the likes.' He poured stew from the can into a biscuit-tin lid and set it down on the ground between us. I felt that I was meant to eat, yet I hesitated. I distrust such kindness, it shakes my lack of faith in human nature. He stopped chewing and glared at me. 'Eat, will you! It's right stuff.'

I ate. After the first mouthful I scuttled away and was sick into the weeds. My fierce friend laughed. I crawled back on all fours and tried another lump of meat. It stayed down. We finished what was on the plate, and he poured out a second helping, and that too we had soon tucked away. It left in my mouth a taste of boiled fur.

'Do you know what that was now?' he asked, wiping his beard on his sleeve. He cackled. 'Monkey stew! Aye, that's right. Up there on the hill by the road I found it, sitting in a tree as cocky as you like eating leaves. A bloody monkey! I nearly broke my neck trying to catch it.' He paused then and frowned. 'Do you know, I'm travelling the roads these twenty year, but I never knew there was monkeys in this country. First I thought it was a bird or something, or a squirrel, but no, it was a monkey all right, I seen them before with them fellows with the hurdy-gurdies, dancing on a string. A tasty lad, though, what?'

He dozed off after a while, sitting bolt upright with his hands on his knees, and I lay back against the wall and nursed my belly as it did its best to digest the remains of Albert, for Albert it must have been, the region could not boast of more than one monkey. How much else of the circus had survived? I had a vision of Mario perched in a tree, munching leaves and gibbering, or of Angel served up piping hot in a can. My friend started up abruptly and grabbed me by the throat.

'*What?*' he roared, '*what?*' I croaked at him and flapped my tongue, and he released me and passed a hand over his forehead. 'Jesus, that was a close one,' he muttered cryptically, and then burst into song.

> O there's hair on this
> And there's hair on that
> There's hair on my dog Tiny
> But I know where
> There's plenty of hair—

He yawned, shook himself vigorously, and rubbed his hands.

—On the girl I left behind me!

His gaiety departed as quickly as it had come, and he began to grind his teeth again, and stared out gloomily at the frozen wood.

'This used to be my place,' he said, jerking a thumb over his shoulder at the wall behind us. 'Cottage I had, grand little spot. Everything I needed, bit of game in the woods there, spuds in the back, a few head of cabbage. There was—' Something occurred to him, and he turned to me and stuck out his hand. 'Cotter's the name. Cotter's cottage, ha!' Before I could shake his paw he clenched it and punched himself on the knee. '*Them fuckers!* Listen, tell me this, what harm was I doing? Christ, didn't they own half the county already, what did they want with my bit of a spot, eh? I had rights, squatter's rights! But O no, O no, the Big House wouldn't have *me* living in their woods, O no! *You'll get shot some day*, he said. *By accident*, he said. Accident my arse. That was the old whore himself, old Simon. Then they come and stove in the roof—and me in the bloody bed there! The fuckers.'

He ruminated for a while in a furious silence, pounding himself with his fist, and then a small light dawned in his eyes and he bared his fangs and grinned.

'But they got their comeuppance too,' he growled, 'aye they did. I heard about it when I was up north, her kicking off in the madhouse, and then your man getting shagged out when her crowd took over. Good enough for them, the mangy bastards. And now I'm back to claim what's mine, my rights, I am.'

I waited for him to calm himself, and then I asked very carefully.

'And what happened to…your man?'

'What? Who?'

'Godkin.'

'Mister Joseph? Fucked if I know. I hear they let him stay on, living in some class of an outhouse.' He glanced at me suspiciously. 'Why?'

'I just wondered.'

'Oo you jast wahndered, did you now? I see, I see.' His teeth were out again, and his eyes gleamed. He clawed at his beard in a paroxysm of suspicion. 'Bejesus, do you know what it is, you talk like one of them yourself. You wouldn't be coming down here to spy on old Cotter, would you, eh? That wouldn't be it, now, would it?'

I backed out of the shelter slowly and stood by the fire watching him. He whipped off his hat and began to beat himself on the thigh with it, and muttered ruefully,

'Dying, says he—like fuck!'

He made a lunge at me and missed and stumbled into the embers of the fire, and as I turned he came up howling and coughing in a cloud of ash. I fled.

'I'll get you! I'll get you!'

At the edge of the wood I tried to leap the ditch and instead fell into it, and when I had crawled up out of the mud to the road I found myself staring into the disenchanted yellow eye of the stuffed tiger in its cage.

I WAS NOT surprised. I had known all along that in the end they would find me again. Perhaps it was that knowledge which kept me alive all that time, against all odds. Now here they were, the silent curtained caravans, the horses asleep in their harness, a life come back to claim me. The attack outside the pub had left bad bruises. Two caravans were missing, and the paint on those remaining was scorched and blistered. Windows were smashed, spokes were missing. A halfdoor hung loose on its hinges like a hand dangling from a broken wrist. The cart on which was carried the tent and tackle was hitched to the last caravan, leaving to one horse the work of two. There was something about the circus standing there silent and deserted that frightened me, a malevolence which I could not understand but only feel, and when Silas himself, hard on the thought of him, appeared around a bend, I crouched and ran to the cart and hid myself on it under a fold of the tent. I heard him shout at someone, and there was a mumbled reply startlingly close to me, and then boots rattled on the road. Mario, I think it was he, pissed against the wheel of the cart. Silas came up.

'Hurry it up now, dear boy, we're on our way. Stirring times, eh ?'

Mario gave no answer, only grunted. They went away, and in a little while we moved off. The sacks under me were wet, I remember that smell, and I remember too the muffled grinding of wheels and the feeling of panic that made my rotten teeth ache as I was carried blindly into the unknown. The journey was brief. We turned off the road on to gravel, and when I lifted the flap and cautiously looked out I saw an open gate which bore the legend,

Lawless House. We crossed the lawn into a field and stopped, and there was a great deal of bustle around me. Surely now they would put up the tent, and I would be discovered, which I think would have been a relief, for I had begun to feel foolish cowering there. But my lair was left undisturbed, and the desire to be discovered left me, and the fear came back. The voices and the bustle receded across the field. I waited for a long time, hearing nothing, and then suddenly there was a cry in the distance and a loud familiar *crack*. Vaguely I had a sense of many feet running over turf, and of storm and panic, of pain, and the voices returned shrill with terror, and Silas gasped,

'Stick her in there, yes, in there—*heave*, damn you!'

They were close to me now, struggling with some heavy thing. I heard Mario blubbering.

'Is she dead?' Sybil shrieked.

'Shut your mouth.'

'O Jesus Jesus!'

'Fuck off!' Mario roared in a voice shaking with mingled rage and hysteria. Silas clicked his tongue.

'My boy, control yourself, and you also, woman. Broken eggs, broken eggs. She'll be all right.'

'She will not, 'Mario muttered. 'She'sa dying.'

'Tut, nonsense. Ah! my, this gore is frightful.'

Again they departed. I could contain myself no longer. I lifted the flap. Angel lay on her back in the open doorway of the caravan in front of me. The top of her head was within inches of my face. Her hair was tangled and her shoulders heaved, and beyond, in the gloom, her hands with the fingers interlocked clutched her heaving belly. There was blood everywhere, in such quantity that it seemed impossible that one body could have shed so much. Suddenly she wrenched her head around and squinted at me.

'You!' she said. 'Ha!'

Her face was set in an agonised grin, but she spoke calmly, with a certain bitter amusement, indifferent to that terrible wound which she held in her hands in there. I wanted to flee, but that great heaving mound of flesh held me rooted to the spot. She turned her terrible grin away from me and said,

'Rats!'

I do not know how long we remained there locked in her dying. Across the field a battle raged. It did not seem real. Tiny figures ran and fought and hopped about, unreal. Rain fell and rattled on the canvas above me, soft spring rain. Angel began to swell, I cannot explain it, she filled the doorway until the posts groaned under the strain, and her massive trunk poured itself into every nook in the caravan, and soon the whole thing was packed with her, throbbing and heaving, rocking on its wheels. She cried out, and rose up in an arch on her heels and head, and upside down her face gaped and turned purple and her hands scrabbled furiously, scampering over her wound like animals. She shuddered and coughed, and all that shook, that flesh, fat, hair, teeth, blood, and she died snarling and laughing, and the spell broke, and I crawled out from my hole.

THE PAST COMES BACK transformed only to startle us with its steadfastness. It is our fractured vision which has transformed it. My broken kingdom all was changed and yet was as it always was. The house was in better repair, and eyed the world through its blazing windows with a steely new assurance, and there were new slates on the roof, and the garden was elegantly barbered, but these trimmings could not disguise the sad fastidious heart of Birchwood, my Birchwood. In the hall the tall clock still bravely tocked. Dead roses scattered amidst bits of a shattered bowl considered their splintered reflections in a mirror laced with cracks. A fat lozenge of sunshine sat on a chair. I could touch nothing, nothing. They had maimed my world. I climbed the stairs to the high window on the landing. Spring sunshine and shadow swept the garden, and the blood gleamed in the grass. The fountain below the window was broken. On the surface of the water a fallen sky trembled. A blue butterfly flickered across the lawn. My fists were wet. I held them up before me and stared at them with stinging eyes, unable to recognise my tears for what they were.

'Make a stir, boy, and by fuck I'll blow your head off.'

It was Cotter, perched like a ramshackle crow in the doorway of the bedroom across the landing with a shotgun clenched against his hip. He spat on the floor at my feet, and without taking his eyes from me he twisted his mouth over his shoulder and roared,

'Lookat here, I have him!'

Silas appeared behind him and stared for a moment, and then smiled, and came at me with open arms. I stepped aside. Cotter lifted the shotgun and aimed it at my head.

'Will I shoot the bugger now?' he asked eagerly of Silas, who waved a white-gloved hand at him and snapped,

'Go away, you, go away!'

He went, banging his boots on the stairs and grumbling, and Silas beamed at me fondly.

'My boy, how are you? I thought you were lost to us forever. Why do you weep? Come, Gabriel, talk to your old friend. You know I never wished you harm. Gabriel?...'

I turned away from him to the window. There were figures moving through the wood, carrying things. Silas saw them too, and sighed and said,

'Burying the dead. Terrible, terrible.' He lit his pipe and then linked his arm through mine, and together we paced up and down the landing. 'It was terrible, Gabriel, truly awful. I didn't expect such...such... None of us expected it, believe me. You've seen those wanton creatures in their dresses? The Molly Maguires, they call them. He led us to believe they were freedom fighters, Gabriel, patriots! Ah, I should have known, but I did not.' He glanced at me sideways and sucked fiercely on his pipe. 'It was all *his* fault, you know. Such...such...'

Such vengeance. From my lair on the cart I saw them drag old John Michael across the lawn and stand him against the glass-house and shoot him in the face with a shotgun. I saw them cut a woman's throat. They beat and kicked and throttled the Lawlesses all to death, and Silas and the circus were in the thick of that slaughter, battling shoulder to shoulder with the Molly Maguires. And I did nothing, nothing. Silas squeezed my arm.

'Come away with us, my boy. We have money now, and the caravans are loaded with provisions. No worries. It's not a bad life, you know, better than staying here. What do you say, eh? Let him have the damn house if he wants it so badly. What good will it do him—or you?' He halted and spun me about to face him and laid his hands on my shoulders. 'Don't be a fool, boy.' I stepped away from him and he dropped his arms. From the garden came a low whistle. Silas glanced toward the window and fixed his eyes on me again. 'Well?' The whistle came a second time. I would not speak. 'Gabriel, Gabriel, you disappoint me. I credited you with wisdom, or at least the base cunning of your class, and now here you are ready to make a fool of yourself for this...this *shambles*!' He peeled off his gloves and offered me his hand, and gave me a last long look in which there was mixed amusement, fondess and reproach. 'Goodbye, my Caligula. We have one last duty to discharge, unpleasant but necessary, and then we are off. I shall not ask you again to go along with us, for I see you're determined. Farewell, my foolish Caligula. Enjoy your inheritance.'

He turned and skipped away down the stairs, pulling on his gloves. I heard him below muttering with Cotter as they went out into the garden, and from the window I watched them set off across the field toward the caravans. Cotter plodded along on his flat feet, and the shotgun, open at the breech, flapped like a flail by his side. Silas was laughing. Even at that distance I could see his fat shoulders quiver. I began to miss him already, the sly old evil bastard. They disappeared behind the caravans, and at that moment the Molly Maguires stepped out of the trees on the drive, three stark men in tattered dresses, with cropped heads and murderous eyes, carrying shovels over their shoulders. They went down to the camp, but as they drew near it Cotter appeared again by the black caravan with the shotgun raised. Here was the last act. The gun roared twice, and two men fell, and a shovel flew up like a spear and glittered in the bright air. Cotter calmly reloaded, and the last of the Mollies turned and ran. The dress clutched at his legs and tripped him, and, as he went down, the third blast, both barrels at once, burst open his head and sprayed the spring grass with blood. The circus moved out. Under the lilacs a figure in a white gown appeared, and a face leaned out into the sunlight and looked up at me with terrible teeth clenched in a grimace and red hair glittering.

I STUMBLED FRANTICALLY around the house barring the doors and windows. I was not trying to lock him out, but to lock myself in. From the kitchen window I peered out across the lawn. There was no sign of him now, but that absence only increased my panic. I found a malevolent friend in a drawer of the dresser, a sleek black knife, a Sabatier. The blade crooned and quivered as I drew it from its wooden sheath and tried the edge against my thumb. I fled with it upstairs to the attic and squatted there in the oniony gloom, moaning and muttering and gnawing my knuckles. The day waned. Rain fell, and then the sun again briefly, then twilight. The tenants of the little room, a brassbound trunk, the dusty skeleton of a tricycle, that stringless tennis racket standing in the corner like a petrified exclamation of horror, began their slow dance into darkness. My face with its staring eyes retreated stealthily out of a grimy sliver of mirror, and then I knew that he was in the house, for I could feel his presence like a minute tremor in the air. I waited calmly. The stairs creaked, and the spokes in the wheels of the tricycle tingled, and the door swung open. Michael, with his legs swaying and the wide skirts falling around him, stood on his hands out on the landing like a huge white mushroom upside down. I could have killed him then, with ease, I even imagined myself flying at him with the knife and plunging it down into his heart, but he was, after all, my brother.

Yes, he was my brother, my twin, I had always known it, but would not admit it, until now, when the admitting made me want to murder him. But the nine long months we had spent together in Martha's womb counted for something in the end. He flipped over on his feet and threw out his arms and grinned, and I picked up the knife in its sheath and pushed it under my belt. His grin widened. He had not changed. His red hair was as violent as ever, his teeth as terrible. I might have been looking at my own reflection. Only his eyes, cold and blue as the sea, were different now. He disappeared. Night fell, blueblack and glossy.

I rattled down the rickety stairs, stumbling in the gloom, and paused on the lower landing and lifted my head and listened. Dark laughter floated up the stairwell. I peered over the banisters. He was down in the hall, juggling with a ball, a blue block and a marble. I started after him, and he fled into the library clutching his dress around him and shedding laughter in his wake, and when I got to the door he had already plunged through the french windows. He danced across the garden like a mad bird, hooting and shrieking and flapping his arms.

In the wood the silver leaves whispered. There must have been a moon, wind, stars. I remember none of them. A pale form glimmered among the trees, but when I swung at it the blade whistled in empty air and the dress fluttered to the ground. Something collapsed under my feet, one of those treacherous hidden caverns in the turf, and I fell headlong into a tangle of thorns. Again that laughter. I lay for a long time with my face in the briars, and he began to sing afar. The anguished evil music settled like black rain on the thorns and trees, the trembling leaves, and soon all of the wood was singing his terrible enthralling song. I went on again on hands and knees. The singing ceased. I came to the edge of the lake. The windows of the summerhouse were faintly lit, and the door was open wide. I crept up the steps. The place was still cluttered with bits of Birchwood's past, deck chairs and straw hats and broken mirrors, but in the midst of it all a kind of lair had been scooped out, and there was a brass bed, and a packing case, and an oil stove and a lamp, a folding chair unfolded. On the bed Papa lay in his black suit and waistcoat with a blue face and staring eyes and a thick protruding tongue. Michael stepped out of the shadows and smiled down upon him faintly.

'Our father, which art dead.'

He looked up at me and the smile faded, and there again in his eyes was that icy white fury as of old. From its sheath I slipped the gleaming panther and clasped it in both hands above my head so tightly that the blade shivered and sang under the strain. He stared intently at the wicked weapon and glided backward slowly, slowly, toward the open doorway, into the shadows, until only his anguished eyes remained, burning in the dark, and at last they too were extinguished. I lowered the knife and spoke aloud my own name seven times and listened to the echoes, and then returned through the wood and across the garden to Birchwood.

I SLEPT THAT night on the billiard table in the study, I do not know why, there were beds enough. At first light I was up tramping about the house. A few chairs had been moved, and Papa's desk with its bundles of unpaid bills was gone, but apart from cavities such as these, and the healed rot and the sound roof, the Lawlesses might never have been. I had to see everything, touch everything, as though by those contacts alone did I exist. Papa would have been proud of my performance, and amused by it. A real son and heir! By the windows in the dining room I halted in a haze of luminous pink light reflected from the garden. The field where the Molly Maguires lay dead was thronged with poppies, the lawn too, blazing blood-red things, terrible and lovely. The dawn was awash with their radiance.

Birds gaily sang about me as I made my way down to the summerhouse. The lake with the sun on it seemed to hover above the ground like something on the point of flight. I opened the shutters in the summerhouse, and there on the floor was that charred patch, Granny Godkin, her mark. My father looked no different by daylight, he was still dead. It was Cotter who throttled him, I think. I cannot be sure of it, but my fierce friend had proved himself an assiduous executioner, and I suspect him before all others. I folded the sheets over Papa and bound him tightly with twine, and dragged that stiff cold larva into the wood. It was a heavy burden, and I made slow progress. In the clearing where the Lawlesses were buried there were more poppies. I thought of burying him there under those flourishing passionate flowers, but although it would have made my task lighter, I had not the heart to plant him among his enemies. Instead I hauled him up the ridge and dug a hole among the birch trees, cursing the rocky ground and the blunt spade and the dead weight that nearly pulled me with it into the grave. I covered him up, and tried to think of a prayer that I might say, not that I thought there was anyone to hear it, but that it might lend a touch of solemnity to this farcical ceremony. All that crimson death sprouting around me in the sparkling green morning had made me light-headed. I could remember no prayers, and so a song, the only one I knew, had to suffice.

> O there's hair on this
> There's hair on that
> And there's hair on my dog Tiny
> But I know where
> There's plenty of hair—

It cheered me up, standing there weeping and giggling, with my hands devoutly clasped, singing for my father. I know that he would have savoured the scene.

—On the girl I left behind me!

There is no girl. There never was. I suppose I always knew that, in my heart. I believed in a sister in order not to believe in *him*, my cold mad brother. No Prospero either, there never is. O but I so wanted to keep that withered wizard, with his cloak and his black hat, stumping on ahead of me always with his stick and his claw and his piercing eyes, leading me slowly toward that rosy grail. Now the white landscape was empty. Perhaps it is better thus, I said, and added, faintly, I might find other creatures to inhabit it. And I did, and so I became my own Prospero, and yours.

I left Papa there to put down what roots he might, and went back to the house. He too had wanted a pet homunculus to comfort him, but what a blow it must have been to realise, with sudden cold clarity—I can see him striking his forehead with his fist—that if Beatrice were to produce a child it would be half a Lawless. And what a mixed relief it must have been to discover that Beatrice was barren, for by the time that fact became plain Martha had come up trumps with her two-card trick. I wonder how many of the family knew of the misalliance between brother and sister? Granny Godkin did, but not Granda. I knew, but denied the knowledge, as Beatrice did for as long as her fractured brain would allow, and then went conveniently mad, and died caged. And Michael? O he knew, yes, yes.

They struck a bargain, Martha and Joseph, admirable in its deviousness, whereby I would stay at Birchwood to be Papa's longed-for son—a *real* Godkin, by god—and Martha would retire with Michael to a secret lair somewhere financed by the Birchwood coffers. There was one condition, namely, that I would be the son of the house, but Michael must be the heir. Agreed! How did they make their choice between identical twin babies? Perhaps Papa shut his eyes and stuck a pin in me, or did Martha see in Michael's puckered face a trace of that cold sly fury and recognise a villian after her own heart? I do not know, but I know that they made the wrong choices, and thereby came their ruin.

I find it incredible that Martha believed her brother to be a man of honour, although he might have been honourable but for his wicked sense of humour. It was not fondness for me, for I was a bitter disappointment, nor hatred for her and Michael, but just an unwillingness to let pass the opportunity of laying the framework for a perfect delayed-action joke that made him, on the very day of their departure, sit down to his desk and carefully inscribe my name into his will. How he must have grinned, crouched there in the gloom of his study admiring that little word and pouring out a brandy. Ah father, I loved you in my fashion.

His plan to lighten with derisive laughter the darkness of his grave went askew, for Martha began to suspect him, and came flying back to Birchwood with her claws out. She found the will, or perhaps he showed it to her, and the battle began. But she was no match for Joe. He brought forward his post humous merriment and laughed at her then. What did she want? Was it that, like me, she had to touch the house in order to believe that she existed? These questions puzzle me still, and many more. Perhaps she only wanted to fight, for while they bickered they hardly noticed that the estate was falling apart. How explain such foolishness? They were Godkins, and no more need be said.

Michael, of course, wanted to be squire, to ride on a black horse around his land and hunt the foxes and thrash the peasants. He wanted all that I had, and hated me for having it and despising it. I think he would have killed me, willingly, it would have been so easy, but something held him back, that same something which stayed the knife in my own hand when we faced each other in the murderous dark of the summerhouse, and so, instead of fratricide, he played with Martha her sly game, and between them they sent me off in search of a sister. But by then all that was Birchwood had collapsed, the Lawlesses were taking over, and Michael too had to fly. Wherever I went he was ahead of me, dogging the steps I had not taken yet. He found the circus, and joined the Molly Maguires, brought them to fight the Lawlesses, and the circus to fight the Mollies. All that blood! That slaughter! And for what? For the same reason that Papa released his father into the birch wood to die, that Granny Godkin tormented poor mad Beatrice, that Beatrice made Martha believe that Michael was in the burning shed, the same reason that brought about all their absurd tragedies, the reason which does not have a name. So here then is an ending, of a kind, to my story. It may not have been like that, any of it. I invent, necessarily.

The weather held for weeks, limpid and bright, wind all day, sun and rain and a luminous lilac glow above the trees, then the evenings, night and stars. At first the silence troubled me, until I realised that it was not really silence. A band of old women came one day and took away the bodies of the dead men down in the field. I watched from my window, fascinated. I wanted to go and help them, to say, *Look, I am not my father, I am something different*, but they would have run away from me, horrified. The poppies languished. I worked on the house, cleared out the attic, boarded up the windows smashed during the siege, tended the flowerbeds, I do not know why. The summerhouse was invaded by pigeons, starlings, a hive of bees. I let them stay there. They were alive, and I had enough of death. Perhaps I shall leave here. Where would I go? Is that why they all fought so hard for Birchwood, because there was nowhere else for them to be? Outside is destruction and decay. I do not speak the language of this wild country. I shall stay here, alone, and live a life different from any the house has ever known. Yes.

The kitchen still bore traces of Josie's peculiar odour. I wondered if she had been a part of those rights which Cotter had come back to claim. I doubt it. She had slipped into a crevice in time and lain there until forgotten. I could no longer remember what she looked like. How many have I lost that way? I began to write, as a